Humanity H2O
RADNOTI X

Dani J. Caile

LINE BY LION
PUBLICATIONS

Preface

2358 AD. After revealing a hideous truth about humanity while surviving a pandemic, escaping death with a brain implant, and murdering both her work partner and the person who saved her from death, Police Officer Karina Reif needs to decide what exactly comes next. Decrypt the vaccine code and save humanity from extinction or disappear from the face of the known universe?

A claustrophobic, subtly humorous, psychotic future of people who no longer know why.

007

SILENCE. The damn silence. With all the to and fro of the last few days, what got to Karina the most was the absence of any sound other than her heart beating. And being alone. Yeah, that was a biggie. On a whole planet that used to have a captive population of thousands, she was now the sole person left alive. If you called this living, with half your brain a computer implant and your body trying to recover from being dead for months. *You are alive.* Thanks. And no high. She missed that high. No more Boroka 357s for her.

Okay, the implant was the reason she was still breathing, but it was also the reason for her cold turkey. As she sat in the shuttle bay on a foldaway plastic chair next to the huge water shuttle with her body shaking from her body temperature dropping due to drug withdrawal on a scorchingly hot desert sandball shithole of a planet, she wondered what her next step was. *A prediction program could be used to analyse your situation.* Seeing as she wasn't at her best, Karina gave it a thought. Why not? Why think when you had a computer in your head? She had no energy for it herself at the moment. Alrighty. *Attach the tablet for you to peruse the results.* Aren't you the pushy one? She ran into the cockpit of the shuttle, dodging the squishy, bloody parts of those inside, and grabbed some cables and a portable monitor. Relieved to sit back down on the deck chair in the bay, she connected her brain implant to Pukanszky's old tablet to show the options available to her.

"So what have you got?" *It would take some time to break the code to extract the vaccine information from the device.* The monitor showed the results. Some time? One hundred and three years? That's a long time, not 'some'. *Time is relative.* Not to me. Although she had access to the tablet itself, the area of the drive which held the vaccine was locked. What had G.D. done to it? Although it was Pukanszky's, Karina also had access to it and all its wonders. But now... "Oh come on! Surely you can do better than that." *Who is Shirley? Name not found.* "Comedy now, huh? Anyway, what is your name? Aren't you me now? Or am I you?" *Are we back to dealing with existentialism or is it possible to show you some options as to your present predicament?* Show me. The monitor threw up a long list which seemed to scroll on forever. "Hey, hey! Hang on! I didn't mean every damn thing! I'm sure I saw 'Download Flappy Bird from the main database' there! Keep it to the essentials, you know, like how to get this vaccine data off the tablet and decoded in my lifetime, and how to get off this damn planet. Those are what I'd call important right now." The list shortened dramatically. "Wow, now that's what I call running out of options. Are you kidding?" There were three. "Thank you. You're a great help. Not. How many billions of instructions can you process in a second?" *Anywhere from thirteen to fifty.* "And this is what you came up with?" *Affirmative. As a shortlist for the short term. 'Flappy Bird' was still in the top ten. It is a classic.* Give a child a spade and he'll dig a hole. "I could've thought of these." *You did.* "Now who's talking existentialism?" The implant went silent. "Three options?" *Basically, yes. Option four was considered but it is 'Shirley' not to your liking. It includes a chair, a chairsaw and some rope.*

"Uh-huh, that would cut things a bit short. For sure. So,

option one: find a skilled hacker. Really? Can you see any around? Hello! Any hackers out there?" Karina listened, to prove her point. "Nope. Thought not. Option two: wait for assistance. That hasn't worked out so well, now has it? How many people tried to rip out my brain?" *Technically they were accessing data.* Shut up. "Option three: learn how to pilot the water shuttle... yes, it's the only way off this shitball of sand without help. If only G.D. had completed putting in the turbines..." *The shuttle is operational but not at an optimal functional performance. It has three turbines and it needs four to function correctly.* "Yes, I just said that. Well, G.D. blew up that last one with his refitted emergency vehicle. So it flies..." *Yes, but...* "...but how can I learn how to fly?" *The database usage is at two point six percent. There is nothing you could not learn.* "I'm sorry, what?" *Connect to the mainframe.* Karina unplugged the cable from the tablet and connected the implant to the main monitor. A surge of heat swam through her head and links lit up and cooled throughout both the implant and what was left of her own brain. Suddenly, she felt the power. "I know kung fu." *Technically, you know the hypothetical moves of Wing Chun, Zi Quan, Xing Yi and Tai Chi Quan but you have yet to practise them.* "Oh. But hey, this is cool." *Would you now like to know how to pilot a water shuttle?* "Sure. While you're at it, put in a few other vehicles." *Affirmative.* "Oh, and can you find the recipe for Goi cuon? I've heard it's pretty moreish and I'd like to try and make it some time." *Any more requests?* "Erm... skateboarding. I never got the hang of that."

For the next few minutes her head felt like a baked potato left in the oven too long. She was sure she smelt smoke, too. After a time, the processing ceased and she slumped back into her chair. "Wow. I can see why people get these things," she said, tapping on the side of her head. *Careful. The installation did not go without its problems.* "Sorry. Hey, teach me all about computing, then I can deal with you." *Is that a threat?* "It could come in handy." *A cooling period is needed. When an appropriate time is available you will be informed and installation of the requested data will proceed.* "Okay. No worries. I have time."

With all this new knowledge in her head, she was hungry, and she picked up the remaining chunk of meat left over from the last meal she'd made in the canteen a few hours earlier. Selecting a collection of music from the mainframe, she downloaded and played it randomly through the loudspeaker of the shuttle bay. Some distorted instrumental music blared through the empty space.

"Now let's go clear up that shuttle. Any ideas how to get rid of blood stains?" *Hydrogen peroxide or Sodium chloride.* In English? *That was in English.* What are those? *Salt will do.* Forget it. Karina unplugged herself from the cables connected to the monitor and begrudgingly walked over to the water shuttle to clear up the bloodbath inside the cockpit.

As she was about to enter the lower hatch, the tablet pinged, the sound echoing through the bay. "What now?" She walked back over, thankful she still had her enhancement suit on, which was working at...wait for it... *Minimal levels...* Thank you. She picked up the tablet and it showed the message: 'Incoming vessel'. What! Not again! ...well, what did she expect? For people to forget that the vaccine was there? That would be unthinkable.

002

AFTER assessing the trajectory data from the tablet, Karina could see the vessel entering the atmosphere was moving at too fast a rate to be able to slow down quick enough to land safely. It looked like a kamikaze strike on the planet. The vessel was also a two-seater, fighter-class. It could have been either military or state. Whichever, whoever, it didn't matter, someone had been sent to collect the vaccine. When would it end? Stupid question.

Karina headed out into the desert — she was getting used to it — with a laser rifle, binoculars and a six pack of beer. She also had on some cool shades she found in Nemes' left breast pocket to save her eyes from the scorching suns. Now with the information from the tablet that had shown her the expected impact area to be only a few kilometres out, she started her squeaky enhancement suit jog across the sand. *Move slightly to the left.* She realigned her run and grabbed the binoculars now hanging from her neck, surveying the sky for any object. And there it was, a tiny dot but pretty hard to miss, what with the flaming tail and smoke emanating from the back of the small vessel. She increased her pace and staggered on.

At about three hundred meters up, well, that's what the binoculars said, the ejection seat popped out of the fiery object and after a moment of weightlessness as the thrusters gave in and gravity took over, the seat fell as the person was released and the parachute opened. Definitely only one to deal with. Maybe there were two, who knew. The small vessel crashed into the desert, sending up a cloud of sand, quickly followed by an explosion. Well, one survived. The ejection seat then unfortunately disappeared from view as it also hit the sand, hidden by dunes. Karina took off, letting the binoculars hang as she jogged towards the still floating dome, which moved away from the landing site due to some strong heat winds off the sand. Every few seconds she stopped to look through the binoculars, and although she was closer, the parachute obscured her view of the person below.

Keeping up the jog, she looked ahead, checking the landscape. Sand, what else? There was a slightly higher dune over to the left, so she headed for it while swinging the laser rifle across her shoulder and getting ready to aim. *Wait for the parachute to fall to the sand, then head for high ground.* Okay, will do. She changed her direction again, though moving slower. Whoever it was could already see Karina approaching on this sparse, open terrain. *Down!* She dived forward as a laser shot flew over her head. She smelt something burning — it was her backpack. The laser shot had gone clean through the six pack! She got rid of the whole pack. What a waste of beer. Not the best, but it was at least wet.

Now on the sand, she could no longer see the parachute, and vice-versa. She took the opportunity to roll and scarper for the higher ground on the left.

In position, she poked the end of the rifle over the top edge of the dune and looked through its telescopic sight. There, some two hundred meters away was a small dark area in the sand, the parachute, half-buried. A path in the sand led to... someone in uniform... an armed police officer running to the next dune on the right. Police officer? Karina aimed for the legs and fired. The officer went down with hands flailing, their firearm dropped, rolling down from their position. Karina took the chance and sprinted as fast as her suit could take her to the splayed out body in the sand. The uniformed officer tried to get up but one of their legs failed them and they went face down into the sand once again. Karina stood over the body, rifle aimed at the back of their head.

"Don't shoot!" said a female voice. "MTSG! I'm here to help!" Karina banged her rifle's muzzle into the person's helmet. "It's me, Borsodi! Don't shoot!"

"Borsodi?" Karina took one hand off her rifle and ripped the helmet off her captive. And there she was, Borsodi, an old acquaintance from her Academy days. Well, what do you know? It's a small universe. Calling her a friend would've been a stretch, though, more like someone she'd once known. It was difficult to make friends at the Academy, all trying to do and be better while pranking and tricking each other into stupid and dangerous situations. Those that did well got the cushy jobs on Earth, huge cuts and easier steps up the ladder to promotion and a larger piece of whatever corruption was going around. Karina hadn't been one of those lucky few — her father was the one connection working against her. Borsodi hadn't been lucky either, but if she remembered correctly, she'd got a better placement than Karina. "What the hell are you doing here? And why did you shoot at me?" Karina kept that muzzle in her face.

"I... I didn't recognise you."

"What? Don't tell me it was the glasses!" She pushed them back up her nose. They weren't really her thing. Practical but they didn't suit.

"Partly."

Knocking Borsodi out would've been Karina's first choice if they weren't stuck out in the desert, as dragging her back would be a pain. "Why are you here?" If it wasn't obvious.

"For the suntan, what else?" Karina watched as Borsodi carefully took out a bandage from her belt and allowed it to seal around the wound on her leg. "How are you? Long time no see!"

"Get up!" Borsodi slowly stood up.

"What, no 'Hi, Borsodi, wow, it's been a while! What's new?'" said Borsodi, trying to smile but it looked like a pained grin.

"What? Who are you to me? Who sent you? I should shoot you, get rid of your sorry arse!" Borsodi held her hands up in surrender but kept her mouth shut. Was she yet someone else to kill before dusk? What was this all about? "Ah, hell! Get moving! Let's go!" Limping, Borsodi did as Karina commanded. It was going to be slow getting back to the shuttle bay, but they had all the time on this world. Who was counting?

003

THE walk back was tiresome and silent save for the sound of the wind blowing sand across their path, scratching their faces. Once back in the shuttle bay, Borsodi went straight for Karina's foldaway chair and sat down, taking off the bandage and inspecting her left leg. It had worked okay coming back, but there was a large cut on her left thigh.

"Oh, that's gonna leave a scar," Borsodi said.

"Make yourself at home, then." Karina replied, aiming her rifle at Borsodi while flipping open another chair from nearby. Borsodi put her hands up again.

"Hey, I'm here to help, remember? And I see you've got your own scar," nodding to her implant.

"Help? All I remember is your words don't match your actions. They've showed something else so far. And as far as I recall, you never helped."

"Okay, okay, I'm sorry. I was a bit jumpy. So would you be if you'd had to fly through a small military fleet to get here. I almost didn't make it," said Borsodi, dropping her hands now and looking around the place. She spotted an open beer can next to the chair and picked it up.

"A what?"

"The blockade."

"What blockade?"

"The military have put a blockade around this system, a drive immobiliser to stop anyone getting in," stated Borsodi. "They think the best thing to do is seal it up." She looked at her leg. "You know, put a plaster on it and it'll go away."

"And why are you here? Specifically you."

"Didn't you get the message from Headquarters?" Karina remembered something about that. It seemed an eternity ago.

"You're a bit late."

"Well, I had some trouble with that blockade. Thankfully the Karina Virus hit the military quite bad, so…" started Borsodi.

"I'm sorry, what?"

"The Karina Virus, it hit the mil…"

"They named the virus after me?"

"Well, they've only just been using that name since it broke in the media a few months ago, but yeah." What? What was wrong with people? She had nothing… she had only a little something to do with the virus!

"It's not my virus, it's Hadudi's, or Hadidi's, whatever, that scientist, not mine."

"History rewritten, eh? Some people get cities, planets and stars named after them. You got a virus," chuckled Borsodi. "Typical Reif, getting the rough end of the stick."

"The Karina Virus…"

"Look at it this way, most people die in obscurity, at least you've got your name on something. Me, I have a beer." Borsodi lifted the can up and drank, giving a face when she swallowed.

"What, at least I have my name on the deadliest virus to hit mankind, a virus that might even wipe it from the entire known universe, you mean?"

"It could have been worse… well, no, probably not. That's probably the worst that could've happened. You've got a point there." Karina could see Borsodi didn't like her drink.

Why should she? It wasn't beer.

"But… but why you? Why did you come? Why not someone else?" Why had Borsodi come to get her? Why not another officer?

"They ordered me to. What? You think I want to be here? I had a good job back on Szergyar 22, got a good cut, too. And a lot of action." She winked at Karina and stared at her head. "So what happened to you?"

"You don't know?"

"Looks like you've been through the wars."

"What are we, friends or something?" They both looked at each other. Karina couldn't recall a single good connection between them. "Yes, I have. I died once." *Four times.* "What?"

"Sorry?" asked Borsodi. "What what?"

"Err… nothing." What do you mean 'four times'? *Unfortunately the particular details are unavailable at this given time, though the motherboard states that your biological vehicle died four times while integration was in process.* Mother…

"So you died and came back… like that?" Borsodi pointed to the implant.

"Yeah."

"I'd rather die. I've heard about those things. And talking of dying, it was strange, and lucky how the virus hit the military so hard." Karina thought of the ol' love triangle, Nemes, Tomez and Develich, now resting together in the cockpit, fluids mixing for the first, last and only time. Fluids.

"Yeah, well, it's only passed through liquids, so… it can get a bit lonely in space, can't it?" said Karina.

"Are you…? Are you insinuating that… sexual intercourse is rampant in the military?" asked Borsodi, shocked.

"From what I've experienced in the last few weeks, anything is possible. The military is kinda filled with people trying to prove how manly they are, or those seeking power over others. Sort of a minefield for orgies, don't you think? Join the military! Prove your manliness by shooting a gun, killing people and ignoring those urges to wrestle your best pal onto the floor using only tongues!"

"What have you been doing these last few years?" Borsodi sat back, trying to get as far away from Karina as it was possible sitting in a chair.

"Not much. Taking my cut, doing drugs, drinking, dying and being forcefully given someone else's brain implant to find a vaccine for a lethal virus." Borsodi took another swig from the can, gave another disgusted face and put it down.

"Not much, then. Oh, so the vaccine's in the implant?" The cat's out of the box? It would die if she opened it. And she'd opened it.

"Didn't you know? I thought that was common knowledge for all visitors to Gubacsi Dulu," said Karina, trying to bluff it.

"Headquarters only told me to retrieve you before the military nuke the planet. But they haven't yet. And now I know why. Skeleton crews."

"Yeah. Nuke? Oh."

"So, not only are you known as the instigator of the virus, you're also the holder of its cure?" said Borsodi. "That's just wrong."

"It's not my virus."

"So you keep saying. I guess it's not your vaccine, either."

This was getting nowhere. Karina dropped her rifle on her lap and sighed. "What now, Borsodi? Your fighter's gone. How are you meant to get me to Headquarters?" Borsodi turned to the water shuttle.

"Is that working?" she asked.

"As far as I know it is." *It is not working at its optimal performance.* "I know."

"You know what?"

"I… know… that it is possible to fly. I learnt how to pilot this thing only this morning."

"How is that possible?"

"With the thing in my head."

"Amazing. Though I'd still rather die than have it."

"That can be arranged," said Karina, raising her rifle again. What now? Cleaning! "But first, the cockpit needs a little clean-out."

"What do I look like, a cleaner?"

"No, you look like someone with two empty hands and no gun. Now get moving, there are some bodies to move."

"What?"

"You'll see."

004

BORSODI was just about to climb into the cockpit when she gave a shriek. Yeah, the cockpit wasn't the best site in the world, with blood and bodies everywhere.

"What are you, squeamish? That's not very professional, Officer Borsodi," said Karina.

"What the hell is that?" Karina was expecting to see some dismembered limb or lump of flesh when she got closer but… it was a piece of lander meat.

"It's lander meat. Haven't you seen lander meat before? They're kinda like kangaroos but…" Karina jumped. "What the f…!"

"Exactly!" They both watched as the small lump of lander meat… moved. Borsodi put her head closer to it.

"Careful!" What did she care?

"It's got some kind of fungi on it," said Borsodi.

"Fungi? We need one of them 'round here." Borsodi gave Karina a face for trying the joke. "Hang on, I'll check the database." *Unknown entity.* What do you mean unknown? *Do not touch it.* What, you think that if you don't say that, I'm going to touch some dead fungi-covered meat that's slowly crawling across the floor?

"What is it?" asked Borsodi.

"I don't know, it's not in the database." She popped her head into the cockpit and saw all the bodies inside. They too had this strange fungi on them, growing over the empty, dry open wounds. "Looks like we'll need some protective clothing for this job," said Karina. "It's definitely not safe to touch this stuff."

"You're telling me!"

"Yes. I am." This fungi looked extremely dangerous. Why didn't anyone know about this stuff? Space exploration used to be about finding new species of flora and fauna but there was nothing in any databases about anything except businesses and how profitable each planet could be due to its mineable resources. Always about the profit. Where was the curiosity, the search for knowledge? Lost in the grip of a coin.

Karina walked over to the compartments at the back of the shuttle bay and soon enough she found what looked like two hazmat suits. They'd do.

Once suitably clothed, Karina and Borsodi dragged the bodies, bagged up the pieces and piled the band of dead heroes and villain up outside the bay on the sand and burnt them. Borsodi squeezed some flammable fluid onto the pile to help the fire, and the flames grew, escaping into the air.

"Hey, have some respect, they… never mind." Karina remembered how these people had treated her, like some object to barter with. She thought about G.D. and his rotting corpse far away on the sandy surface and wondered which got to him first, the landers, termites or this fungi?

"We'll need to disinfect the cockpit now, it might not be safe to enter without these," said Borsodi, pulling on her plastic suit.

"Who's 'we'?" Karina tapped on the pistol hanging in her holster.

"Oh come on, I've already said I'm here to help, you don't need to hold me up at gunpoint," pleaded Borsodi.

"But you are helping, you're disinfecting the cockpit so

we can leave. And who's holding you? You can go if you want."
Karina pointed out to the desert. "You're free to go."

Borsodi sighed and walked back into the shuttle bay.
"Where can I find some cleaning equipment?"

"One of the doors at the back somewhere, I don't know.
What do I look like, the cleaner?" Karina watched the fire as the
bodies began to break apart, collapse and turn to ash.

"I can't say what you look like. Your bald head has a
kind of a purple shine to it."

That was strange. Her natural mousey hair should be
coming through after that last dye. *Integer recalibrated.* What?
You can change the colour of my hair? *The sebaceous glands are in
close proximity and some alterations can be suggested to particular
follicles.* That is crazy. *Are you planning on flying the water shuttle?*
Yes. *It is not advisable.* Are you worried I'll crash? You taught me
how to fly it. *No, it is not your theoretical knowledge or lack of real
experience which is at fault, it is the operation of the vehicle itself.*
What's wrong with it? *There are only three turbines as opposed to
four.* And? *Four are needed.* Oh come on!

"Can you give me a hand?" shouted Borsodi, standing
there with one disinfectant tank strapped on her back and
another in her hands for Karina. "The quicker we do this, the
quicker we get off this planet!" We. She'd been on the planet
less than an afternoon and it was already 'we'. Typical Borsodi.
Karina thought she should leave the bitch here.

"Alright!" *You cannot fly the water shuttle.* "Just watch
me!"

"What? Why?"

"Nothing." *You cannot fly the—* Shut up.

005

"COUNTDOWN in five, four..." *You cannot fly the—* Oh who cares. Karina hit the big red 'engage' button and held onto the steering column as the turbines began to spin and create lift. Piloting one of these wasn't so difficult, more a 'point and fly' type deal. But then, did you really have to be such an egghead to be able to fly? And was she really going to fly? Most of what was running through her head now were instructions on how to fly the thing on autopilot.

However, she sat there in the pilot's seat wearing a brand new, and with an emphasis on clean, AxiCorp uniform she'd found in a locker while Borsodi sat in the co-pilot, twiddling about with the console in front of her, trying to get up some star charts. Karina had kept her busy by delegating that task and the girl seemed happy with it. Pulling the brake levers slowly forwards, and the steering straight back, they drifted out of the shuttle bay and into the blinding rays of the suns.

"Ahh!" shouted Borsodi, hiding her eyes with her arms.

"Sorry, old habit," apologised Karina, hitting a few buttons which shaded the cockpit viewscreen. The water shuttle ran smooth. What was the implant's problem? Three turbines worked. Sure, there was the occasional alert from the controls that something wasn't quite right, but nothing that the manual she'd learnt from didn't allow to ignore. "Are you ready?" she asked as she strapped herself in. Borsodi did the same and nodded. "So you're taking me somewhere. Exactly where are we going?"

"To Headquarters. I'll punch it in once we're in orbit."

"Oh, okay. Did you eat much today?" she asked.

"No, why?"

"Because… this." Karina hit the thrusters and they both felt the Gs as the water shuttle shot up through the air and watched the blue sky turn to black as the stars grew brighter. Karina was sure she heard a pop as they cleared the atmosphere of Gubacsi Dulu and entered space. A relief dropped her shoulders as the Gs and the thought of being on that planet lessened. She was finally off! Free from the sandball shithole! All that had happened before vanished in a moment.

Once the Gs had come down and become bearable, she looked over at Borsodi, who was now a little whiter but seemed okay. "How was it for you?" *This was not a suitable solution to your problem.* "What?"

"Mmm?" asked Borsodi, lost somewhere in her head.

"Nothing," she said, smiling.

Perhaps you should have downloaded water shuttle engineer first class. "I'm sorry, what?"

"What did you say?"

"Nothing. Erm, sorry, I speak to myself a lot nowadays."

"Oh, that's okay. Me, I only speak to certain parts," replied Borsodi, now completely aware and running through some star charts, and selecting the destination. Karina didn't want to know which parts she was talking about.

So, what was she saying? The water shuttle seemed to be running well, there were no problems… except for that little red light, and that one, and that one… *There is a reason why a water shuttle has four and not three turbines.* Oh, really? *The third and fourth turbines are balanced in usage to correlate for any errors in the software driver due to the extreme weight and stress on the vehicle.* What are you telling me? *If you do not find a destination soon, the third turbine will explode, quickly followed by the other two.* And then? *Then you are... 'afloat', floating, a floater...* in the toilet that is space? I get it, we'll be up shit creek. *Affirmative.* "Borsodi?"

"Yes? Got it!" She pressed one last button, entering their destination and sat back happy and content. "Is this the light speed drive activator?" she asked, nodding over to a large orange button.

"Yes, but don't push it just yet."

"Why?"

"Just how far is it to Headquarters?"

"Oh, quite far. But we'll be there soon. Plus the military are only stopping shuttles from coming IN to the system, not going out. They don't expect that."

"Right, that's nice to know. And, if you don't mind me asking, where's the nearest colony or base?" asked Karina, watching the energy bars on the three working and installed turbines.

"Why?"

"Because the turbines are about to explode."

"Oh." Borsodi looked ahead for a moment as she must've only heard some of that. "What!" Her face turned white. Again. "Why are the turbines about to explode?"

"Apparently three turbines aren't enough for a water shuttle."

"What? What do you mean, three? Isn't that enough? And why didn't you tell me something was wrong with this shuttle?"

"It didn't seem important."

"Didn't seem important?!"

"Nope. Look, we're going to be dead in space if we can't find a nearby planet to land on," Karina said. The third turbine energy bar was already reaching into the red danger zone and they'd only gone a few thousand kilometres from Gubacsi Dulu.

"Are you kidding?"

"Nope." A red light flashed throughout the cockpit.

"Oh come on, it's only a warning light. Where's the siren?" asked Borsodi, laughing it off.

"On mute." Karina hit the button and the siren matched the light, killing their ears. Karina turned it off. "I gave you the star charts. Be useful and find something quick." There was a jolt as they passed something in space. The sensors showed a military destroyer, parked up. It's trajectory changed and it turned towards them.

"Oh crap!" Borsodi opened up the star charts once again and flicked through those systems closest to themselves. "Not one bloody base, not one bloody colon..." The red light flashed quicker while the siren grew stronger. Karina watched as turbine number three lost all power. There was a small vacuum 'whumph' sound behind and below them as it exploded. The military destroyer was beginning to follow.

"About now would be a good time to find somewhere," said Karina as the two remaining turbines energy bars began to rise.

"Okay, okay... hang on..." Borsodi moved through different menus and charts. "Shit."

"What?"

"It doesn't have to be a working one, does it?"

"What, colony? No!" The military destroyer had already matched their speed.

"Okay..." She pressed a final button and the destination was set. Karina heard a two second countdown and the light speed drive kicked in. As did the G-force. It felt like a twenty. *Eight. The shuttle buffers its passengers.* She looked over at the console and the turbine energy bars hit maximum and began to increase. "We're almost there."

"Where?" The two turbines flickered out and exploded in unison, releasing both of them from the G-force and back into normal space. Small consolation.

"A small abandoned mining colony on Radnoti X, only six light years away from our departure," said Borsodi. "Problem is, its data file has a toxic warning all over it. It says it's not advisable to go there."

"How toxic is it?"

"Apparently no one's been there since it was left to rot."

"Well, I'm not an expert but from what I can see from the readings... we at least made orbit," said Karina, rechecking the monitors as they drifted closer to a planet.

"I guess that's a good thing," Borsodi smiled as she looked over the monitors herself. Karina saw something which might kill that smile quickly.

"Yes and no. We got there, but we'll also be crash landing once the gravitation of the planet pulls us down through the atmosphere," she said.

"So we're crash landing into a toxic planet?" asked Borsodi. The smile had died. Prediction correct.

"Something to look forward to," replied Karina, bringing back the smile on her own face. Out of one fire and into another. Looking over at Borsodi, Karina tried to remember anything about this woman. Nothing. Not one thing came back from those Academy days. But she was sure quick to smile. Easy to please or a smile of manipulation? Did she care? Nope.

006

OTHER than the large warships and destroyers within the military, and possibly a few luxury yachts owned by the heads of AxiCorp, water shuttles were up there with the biggest, possibly the biggest self-contained shuttles in company space. Mining barges were just boxes, large containers orbiting the planet while smaller shuttles went back and forth with small loads from the surface. The price of the energy needed for a shuttle that size to take off from a surface would be more than the barge held. It was more cost-efficient this way, but now Karina knew why water shuttles were different. A gruesome truth, a heinous, disgusting truth.

Another was that they were losing altitude at quite a fast rate. Nice view of the tops of the clouds. How long was it until they crashed on the surface of this planet? *Two minutes and thirty-two seconds.* Thank you. What if we jettisoned all the water? *Two minutes and twenty seconds.* Thank you, gravity.

"Hey, Borsodi, what is this place again?" asked Karina.

"Radnoti X, an old mining site is here somewhere, unused. Not that we'll see it."

"So, nothing here but dust and rust?"

"Yeah. And a bit of wind. But at least we have water," said Borsodi, pointing her thumb to the back and their cargo.

"What, this? It's probably all infected."

"No, really?" She was honestly shocked. "Hell, that's a shame. What a waste." If only she knew. "Then we really are doomed. I thought seeing as it all came out of the ground, it would be safe." Ah, how the ignorant live.

"Yeah, go figure," muttered Karina. She wasn't going to burst her bubble. A few messages popped up on her console. Then some more. "That's strange."

"What's strange?" asked Borsodi.

"I tell ya, this is strange, but seeing as we're falling to our deaths, I can take a little strange just around about now. For another minute or so, give or take."

"There…" The clouds parted and Borsodi saw it shoot past the viewscreen, a tiny point of manmade structure in a landscape of mountains. "That's the mining site! And… and there were lights on down there!"

"Meaning?" Karina already knew, the water shuttle's sensors had told her.

"Someone's at home?"

"I hope they're friendly. I'm starting to get tired of hostility." Was she falling into another frying pan of trouble? If the past was anything to go by, yes.

"But there shouldn't be anyone here!" said Borsodi. "It's a toxic area!"

"'Shouldn't be' is only a concept. What 'is' is reality. And it comes in many forms." Where did that come from?

"What are those?" asked Borsodi. The sensors picked up dozens of small vehicles appearing around them.

"I don't know…" Karina flicked a few more switches she 'instinctively' knew to hit. "Tug shuttles. They're usually used to lead large shuttles into bays, but we're falling too fast for them to help, for sure." The tug shuttles, now probably fifty in total reached them, and all around they could hear a multitude of contacts on the lower part of the water shuttle. For a moment there was no difference in their falling trajectory but gradually as the seconds ticked by, their vehicle slowed in its descent. "Apparently they can help," corrected Karina.

Although they were technically still falling, it was a more controlled movement. They also changed direction, being sent back towards the mining site they'd seen as they 'flew' by in a slow diving loop.

"Look, the tug shuttles are moving us into the bay. It's all lit up like it's Christmas!" said Borsodi, pointing to them on the viewscreen. "We're saved!"

"Is it Christmas? What's the date? I can't tell, I've been out of it for so long."

"No, it's just a figure of speech. No one does Christmas anymore," said Borsodi.

"Yeah? But maybe they do. That's a lot of lights." More lights flickered to life as they moved closer. The small mining site came into view in detail, showing its decay and disrepair. A mangled pile of rust sitting between two large outcrops of rock, with no sign of life. But someone had sent out the tugs. Who? "Looks like we're gonna make it."

"Yeah, looks like it! I wonder who's down there?" Borsodi nodded over to Karina's weapon. "I think we'd better be ready, though." She held out a hand for a weapon. Karina ignored her, only grabbing her own.

"Ready," said Karina, checking the charge. There was enough for a quick, short fight if needed.

The huge water shuttle felt like it was resting on cushions as it relaxed down onto a large shuttle pad on the top of an outset building. Karina heard the shearing of rusting steel and concrete as they landed. And then a familiar sound. Footsteps. Steel boots running across metal to be more precise.

"So far, this toxic planet of yours is more alive than it seemed to be. Shuttle tugs, now footsteps?" asked Karina. She jumped up out of her seat with her laser rifle in hand.

"It said it was toxic. Maybe it cleared up?"

"Must've." Karina ran to the cockpit hatch and switched on a surveillance camera. Three bodies in hazmat suits. One of them had a drill, the other two carried some large barrel and pipes. "Three of them. There is life out there, but not as we know it," said Karina. Where was that from?

"What are they doing?" asked Borsodi. The drilling started, so Karina pointed at the noise.

"Time for masks, I think." Karina ran over to some supply cupboards but found them bare.

"It's almost through," warned Borsodi.

"Let's hope the air is breathable." They both watched as the drill came through the fuselage and air escaped outside. "I guess not." A tube instantly popped through the hole and smoke began to fill the cockpit. "Oh, and there I was thinking they were friendly." Karina let off a laser bolt which did nothing except heat up a part of the metal surrounding them. Borsodi hit the deck first, losing consciousness and Karina slowly followed her. *Systems running at minimal levels.* You're telling me. Time ticked on, somehow Karina was still conscious, but her body was down, lying on the deck, her eyes and ears watching and hearing everything. First the people outside melted the lock to open the hatch, then they marched in.

"Hey. This one's a female!" said one of the intruders looking over Borsodi. Why, was it some surprise? Were females a rarity? It was a mining colony. Another hazmat owner came over to Karina.

"I think this one is, too." The cheek of the man! Think? She saw her body being moved around as though her mind wasn't connected. "Yeah, it is!" Hey! *Shutting down.* Wait, not yet. Who are these people, what are they do…?

007

PAIN. Ankles. Her feet were being dragged across the floor and her tied arms were held by someone, probably two people. *Systems on.* She picked up her feet and started tapping out steps. It was cold, not freezing but just cold enough to be uncomfortable. Her Axicorp uniform felt cold on her skin.

"This one's up," said a male voice. "Hey! A little more effort, you!" Karina guessed the remark was directed towards herself, so she started walking. She opened her eyes only to see blackness. A bag over her head. Well, what a welcome! It was something to find someone alive down here, but now what? What fate were they destined for? Prisoners would've been the best of all the options, though unfortunately Karina thought the worst.

"Borsodi!" said Karina, her voice muffled through the bag.

"Be quiet! She's... resting," said a second voice, finishing with a laugh.

"Who are you? What are you doing?" she screamed.

"This ain't the time for questions."

They stopped walking and she heard a door squeaking open. She was pushed through and plonked down on a bench. She heard someone putting something else, probably Borsodi, on something opposite her. The smell of stuffy stale air coming through the bag told her they were in a room which hadn't been used for a while. There were a few shuffling footsteps and the door closed and locked.

"Hey! What about the bag?" shouted Karina.

"Better to keep it on, believe me," said that first voice.

There was a little scuffling noise behind Karina, something moved beside her. Four little feet started running up her leg. "Ahh!" She lunged out, kicking her leg and heard a small animal screech as it hit the opposite wall and then scurried away. *Rattus norvegicus. I guessed that.* "Borsodi?" Karina stood up, hands still tied, and moved over to the other side of the room, only a few metres away and hit the edge of a bench with her shin — a device to find furniture in the dark. She brushed her left knee over the top and instantly found one of Borsodi's legs, with her body lying on the bench. She was breathing but not conscious, or at least not responsive. What had they done to her?

Karina realised her enhancement suit was still on. Why hadn't they taken it off her? She tried to break whatever was holding her hands tied together. Nothing. *Suit operating at minimal levels. I know that, you told me that before. Lie down on the floor.* What? There are rats in here, there's no telling how dirty it is. *Lie down on the bench.* Okay. Why? No answer. She lay on the bench and suddenly she felt the weight of her body and the suit, causing pain throughout her whole body. "That hurts! What the...!" *Redirecting power to upper limbs.* What? *Break the ties.* Karina tried and whatever was holding her hands together snapped. *Stabilising power.* Gradually, her body became lighter and the pain emanating throughout her body stopped. She brought her hands to the front and rubbed her sore wrists. Hesitantly, she took the bag from head. A small cell. Not such a great surprise. One tiny light above and looking at the floor, she was happy she chose the bench. It was cold, though, just like the corridor, with her breath turning to mist. Was that a bone in the corner? Borsodi lay on the opposite bench, tied and with a head bag. Karina couldn't break her ties but took off the bag.

"Ahh!" She jumped back. Borsodi's eyes were open, staring coldly ahead. "Borsodi? You okay?" No response. Karina lay her hand on Borsodi's shoulder and the woman flinched. "Borsodi?" Still nothing. She decided to go and sit back down on her bench. There was nothing else in the room save for the light, the two benches and that bone in the corner. No sign of the rat, but the light didn't reach the furthest corners. Karina dreaded to think what was over there. After a moment, Borsodi turned over and faced the wall, showing her hands tied by some plastic strip. "Borsodi?" The rat made another appearance, running across Borsodi's lying body. One neat flick of the animal into the corner where the bench met the wall and a short, sharp crunch with Borsodi's size 37 steel-toe boots finished it off. Karina decided to give her some time alone with her thoughts. Maybe being tied up would be safer for her at the moment.

Karina headed straight for the door and pushed. It budged, but only a millimetre or so. What do you think? *Electronic lock. Error. No power in the door.* What? It's bolted? *Affirmative. Redirecting power to limbs.* What do I do? *Right foot, 45 degrees, left foot forwards.* What? Oh, right! Xing-Hi push? *Affirmative.* Will it work? *We can but try.* Not Conan Doyle again. *Three, two, one...* Karina pushed, flipping her hip and allowing the push to emanate through her palms and into the door. It moved. Really? It works? *Repeat. Three, two, one...* This time there was the sound of creaking metal behind the door. Another! *Three, two, one...* With a snap of metal, the door slowly opened. Eureka! *Stabilising power.*

"What now?" she said, walking into a dark corridor. Escape? She took a few steps and looked around. Nobody about. "Hey, Borsodi?"

Just at that moment, a man turned a corner ahead, with gun in hand. Damn! There was corridor to her right and she took it, running down it into the darkness. She almost tripped on the first of the stairs but finally was able to fall 'up' them. She heard the steps behind her. A laser shot just missed her.

"Don't shoot! Let her go!" shouted someone.

Karina kept running up, going around the stairs, landing after landing. As she went up, the air grew colder, making her limbs hurt with the exertion. She could still hear steps coming from behind, so she took the first door she saw. Another corridor. She ran down it and took yet another set of stairs going up.

"Keep up with her!" shouted the same guy.

The stairs suddenly stopped. A door was there.

"Don't!" shouted another voice. She guessed the word was for her.

She did. The handle wouldn't turn so she pushed on the door with her shoulder and it opened. She was swept back by the wind and rain pouring in. Without air, water filling her face and a blast of cold air, she lost her breath, her throat burned and she started coughing, lying on the floor. She heard the door close and a few voices spoke.

"Is she going to be alright?"

"Yeah, a few seconds won't hurt her."

Karina gasped for breath. *Shutting down...*

008

WHAT? Where was she? She looked around, only to see the cell she was in before, with Borsodi on the bench opposite, still not moving. Somehow she'd got back. Had she slept? No, she'd 'shut down'. *Affirmative.* You have a habit of doing that. *It is only for your own sake.* Isn't bad for you to shut down. *Affirmative.* Then let me sleep. Karina couldn't remember the last time she'd slept. Okay, being unconscious, plenty of times, thanks to the implant as well, and even though it said so, she was sure it wasn't healthy to be out so many times. *All systems running on minimal levels.* Yeah, right. So why wasn't she sleeping? *Would you like to sleep?* Yes. *'Perchance, to dream'?* Why not? *In your predicament it is not advisable to sleep, and in your condition it is also an unnecessary procedure.* My condition? What am I, pregnant? *The mineral and chemical levels within your body are being sustained correctly. Your physical vehicle is being allowed to relax continuously and in a set defined pattern as you are conscious.* So you're controlling my body intake? *Affirmative.* And my soul? *Define.* My soul, my being, my spirit? Doesn't that get to have a rest? *Please state the location of your soul.* Oh come on! So you can't detect my soul? *I can 'detect' everything that I am connected to, all 30.057 trillion cells within your physical vehicle.* And my soul? *Please define 'soul'.* Don't you know what a soul is? *Soul: the spiritual or immaterial part of a human being or animal.* Yes, that's it. *Please state the location of your soul.* We're going around in circles here. *Please state the loca...* Okay, okay, enough already.

Karina heard the lock open in the door. They must've fixed it. She looked over at Borsodi but she hadn't moved. The door swung open and Karina jumped at the chance, charging at the opening. Take every, and any, opportunity. Unfortunately she was met by a large man wearing a complete military outfit, body armour and all. She was pushed straight back to her bench and found the barrel of a rifle in her face.

"How did she get loose?" asked a man behind. He entered the room and looked at both Karina and Borsodi.

"Maybe it was the suit she's wearing," replied the body armoured man. "Who brought them in? Juhasz?" The other man nodded. The body armoured man looked over at Borsodi. "Let me guess, the other was Bolond?" Another nod. "I'm gonna'ave to have a word with him." He checked his rifle's charge.

"Oh, yes, I see," said the other man. "I think a short, sharp disciplinary action wouldn't go amiss instead. These things shouldn't go unpunished."

"We haven't had one of those in years," said the body armoured man.

"We haven't had guests in years."

"Guests?! Is this the way you treat guests?!" shouted Karina, at the end of the barrel.

The other man sighed and waved to someone outside and two more men came in. One gave a coat to Karina and the other wrapped another around Borsodi's shoulders. "Please accept this with our compliments. You will find this place is a little too cold for your uniform," said the man. The two other men grabbed Borsodi, waking her and walking her out, still tied and bagged. "Take her to the Doc, just to make sure. Bohatch, a moment, please."

"You sure?" asked the body armoured man, Bohatch.

The other man nodded again. This guy liked nodding. Maybe he was a 'yes' man. Karina studied the coat, it was a standard body warmer. It fit well over her enhancement suit.

"I apologise for all that has happened so far. We have to have our... precautions," said the man. "When we see the strange occurrence of an AxiCorp water shuttle falling from space and into our atmosphere, what else can we do." Karina was going to rush him but she caught a glimpse of a taser in his right hand. "My name is Germann, I'm the Number Two around here." He stared at Karina's head. "Ah, now I see what Juhasz meant. You have an implant. How's that working out for you?" He expected an answer?

"Err, fine. It brought me back from the dead," replied Karina. What was she meant to say? Oh, excellent, thank you, it's made my life so much better. And I can add up simple Math now! *Would you like me to do some abstract algebra?* Stop it. Germann sat back a little on the bench.

"Back from the dead? Our analysis of your shuttle's trajectory shows that you made a short jump from Gubacsi Dulu, a place of recent ill repute."

"Yes, there was a minor setback," she replied. Whether she was talking about the shuttle or Gubacsi, even she didn't quite know.

"What, on Gubacsi or with the shuttle?" There you go.

"The shuttle. I wouldn't call what happened there minor."

"Absolutely. Yes, three turbines. AxiCorp was never the one for human rights, safety precautions, or the value of a person over profit." He could say that again. He should say that again. "As for Gubacsi... no, not a 'minor' setback... we are not exactly cut off from what is happening in the universe at the moment. We heard about the virus. And we have quarantined the water on your shuttle. Although water is a precious commodity here in our small community, our small community is more precious than that particular commodity of water." He cleared his throat. "Excuse me for the play on words." He was playing?

"Our shuttle database said no one was here," said Karina. Join the conversation, add some words or two, make it interesting, why don't you.

"Ah, yes. AxiCorp databases. They only tell you what you need to know. Let me guess, 'toxic planet?" asked Germann. A taser swung in full sight, hanging from his belt.

"That's what we got," she replied.

"And I'm assuming this planet wasn't your planned destination?"

"No, it wasn't."

"Nice for you to say so. We've already checked your shuttle's data, by the way. We know where you were heading. But why?"

"I know I'm not dressed correctly, but we're both state police officers. Where else would we be going except Headquarters?"

Germann's movements stopped. "Headquarters? Oh, where?"

"Police Headquarters." What was the problem.

"Oh… right. I see… What is your name?" he asked.

"Don't you already have that?" said Karina.

"Where were we going to get that information? From the shuttle's manifest? You're not the assigned pilot of the vehicle. Not male, 6 foot 10, and you have no moustache." She checked, it had been a while since she'd had a facial. Was it wise to tell him her name?

"You're holding me captive. One of your guys did something to my companion. Why the hell would I tell you my name?" argued Karina. Germann leaned against the doorframe.

"It has been over a decade since we've had any visitors to our small community here. As we all can see, there is a rather large pandemic going on in the habitable universe, one which we have fortunately been able to escape from — until now. You and your companion are the first to appear here since AxiCorp left us to rot on this planet along with its mining facility and the first to appear since the virus outbreak, and you have brought a shuttle filled with contaminated water here from what we've heard was the source of the virus, water from Gubacsi Dulu. Precautions were needed. Unfortunately, we have all suffered, some more than others, and a few of us are a little more... wired than the others. It will be handled appropriately. Now, what is your name? You mentioned the other's name... Borsodi?"

"Yes. Borsodi. My is... Reif."

"Karina Reif?"

"Yes."

A pause. And then his laughter filled the small room. There was a squeak from the corner, another rat. "You are Karina Reif?"

"Well, not the original. I have this thing in my head taking up the space of what was half my brain."

The man wiped away his tears. "We intercepted a few messages regarding yourself. Oh my. Karina Reif."

"What am I, famous or something?"

"Definitely something. Please." He opened the door and

gestured her to leave the cell. "The Doc has already cleared you of having any infection. You are free to come and meet the boss."

"That's not the definition of 'free'," said Karina, poking her head out of the cell and noticing Bohatch waiting outside.

"It's all you're getting for the moment. For your own safety," he sniggered.

"What?" asked Bohatch.

"This is Karina Reif," replied Germann. Bohatch's mouth open slightly and his eyes widened a little.

"No!"

"Oh yes."

Bohatch let go of his rifle's stock and grabbed Karina's right hand in his and shook it once. "Legend." Apparently he was happy to meet her, though he didn't smile. She didn't know how to feel about that.

"Come this way," said Germann. "First off, let's see some justice." Karina followed him down the corridor, with Bohatch behind. He pressed the charge on his rifle and they all heard the hard setting: kill. "Bohatch, really?"

"Eh?" Germann pointed to his rifle and Bohatch looked down. "Oh, sorry." He lowered the charge down a little.

009

THE mining colony, from what Karina could see so far, was a succession of interlocking corridors, mostly underground — there were no windows, for one, and it was a mine. Where else would it be? Small lights a few metres apart lined the ceiling. They'd white-washed the walls to make it brighter but it had turned white-grey over time and in many places there were dirt marks and holes. The place was a dump.

"Get the decorators in at any time?" asked Karina.

"You're not catching us at our best, I admit. You should've come twelve years ago. We had some party back then," replied Germann. A group of smaller people appeared from a corridor and they came up to the man. Karina couldn't make out what they were saying as they gibbered away. Germann nodded his head. "What? You did what?" She heard more of their strange language. She thought everyone spoke universal English nowadays but apparently not. "Speak English. I don't understand what you're trying to say. How many years have you been stuck in this mining colony and you still haven't bothered to learn the language?" More alien-like mutterings. "Go away! Find yourself a translator or something!" Germann pointed down another corridor and they left with their own style of gestures. At least those were universally recognised. "Sorry about that. Where were we?"

"What were they speaking?" asked Karina.

"Mexican, an old Earth language. Out-dated and used in poorer parts of the population, but who else is going to work on a remote mining colony? I know a few words but honestly, you'd thought they'd learn English." They all stood between corridors. "Why are we here?"

"Justice," said Bohatch.

"Yes. Of course. This way." Germann walked down one corridor and then turned back and walked down another. Karina waited for him to make up his mind. Bohatch let his rifle hang down.

"Are you lost?" she asked.

"No, he's always like this," said Bohatch.

"Be quiet." Germann walked down another corridor with more confidence. "This one." They followed. They passed many doors, climbed stairs, and went through a few larger areas which led to other large areas, probably the mines and launching pads, and other facilities. How the hell did she know? There weren't any signs to help find the way around, but they met a few people moving around, busy doing whatever they had to do. No one greeted each other, but when they saw Karina, they paused to look, then continued on.

"Nice community," she said. Small talk gets you everywhere.

"Were you expecting salutes? Even at the best of times that really wasn't the norm here," replied Germann. "This is a mine, we work hard. No time for niceties."

"What happened? Why did AxiCorp put this place down as toxic?" she asked.

"A short story, really. We became unprofitable. The last shuttle out took all that was of value and left with the promise that there'd be another to pick us all up and take us to the closest recruiting facility. That shuttle never came."

"How long ago was that?"

"Nineteen years," said Bohatch.

"What have you been doing for nineteen years?"Germann ignored her question and kept walking.

"I've been in the gym," said Bohatch, showing his 22 inch right bicep. She would've thought he was flirting if it wasn't for the deadpan facial emotion.

"Good to know you've used the time well," said Karina. With sarcasm. She followed Germann, leaving Bohatch to his flexed bicep.

"Veres!" Germann had found someone in the corridor he was willing to speak to. "What does the Doc say?"

"He says it's positive." The new man looked over at Karina and nodded a greeting.

"Ah, this is Veres, our administrator, he does all the paperwork, knows all the news and rumours. If you need to know something, go to him," said Germann. "Veres, this is Karina, Karina Reif."

"You have got to be joking," said Veres. "THE Karina Reif?"

"As original as can be, apparently," she replied. Germann pointed to the implant. Veres tried to touch it but Karina flicked his hand away.

"Sorry. Just curious," apologised Veres.

"So, it's positive," said Germann.

"Yes. We have him in Room 128. Everything is ready."

"Room 128? That's the one next to the sewage system?" asked Germann.

"Yes, it's not used much, that's why we chose that one."

"Okay." Germann turned to Karina. "Apparently your companion will get justice today. The room is only a few corridors away. Are you ready to witness the procedure?"

"Procedure? What happened to Borsodi?"

"Come now, you saw how she was. Bolond is not one of our strongest, in mindset. This way." Germann continued to lead the way, now with Karina, Bohatch and Veres in tow. It took a few more minutes to get to the particular room, and Karina could hear the shouts of a man inside.

"I'm the victim here! I've been locked away for so long, we've all been locked away here with nothing! Nothing! I'm a victim of the system!" shouted the man. Germann opened the door and the place went silent. A man was chained to the opposite wall, arms outstretched. Karina saw both fear and anger in his eyes, switching every few seconds.

"Bolond, you've been found guilty of the crime. You know the price," said Germann. Bohatch pushed Karina into the room and motioned her to sit down. Once sat, she realised Borsodi was there, too, sitting a few seats away. She was glancing into space at nothing.

"Screw you, Germann! She... she was asking for it! I... I was doing her a favour!"

Germann nodded over to another man. "Juhasz, you are an accomplice to the crime. It is your duty to carry out the punishment." Juhasz was holding some large, heavy cube which had two handles attached on either side.

"Don't you dare, Juhasz! Don't listen to him! Juhasz!"

Karina could see the man didn't want to do it, but those present were pressuring him. He stepped towards the chained man and placed the large cube over the front part of Bolond's lower torso. Juhasz pressed a button on both handles and without a scream... something happened. Juhasz removed the cube and the chained man hung his head.

"What just happened?" whispered Karina to Bohatch who was the closest.

"He just got neutered. Best thing, really," he replied. "No more trouble now."

Karina sat and watched the men move over to the chained man as they either said something to him or touched him, patting his shoulder or giving him a soft slap on his face. The man, Bolond, looked at peace, tired but at peace. Germann's face came into view.

"Now we go see the boss," he said, gesturing her to follow. Bohatch helped her understand it wasn't a choice. She took one more look over at Borsodi before leaving, but she was still non-responsive, staring ahead into space.

"What about Borsodi?" she asked.

"The Doc will deal with her, don't worry. He knows what to do," said Germann. "Now, come."

010

THEY all took a lift down to some lower level, which one she couldn't see because the lift panel was obscured by Bohatch, but at least Germann didn't need to lead them through any corridors. The lift doors opened to a large area filled with light and sound, soft, natural noises soothing to the ear. Karina had to blink a few times. There were plants down here, growing on or near the walls, and a constant chirping of something, an animal?

"The menagerie," said Germann. "Or at least a Radnoti X meagre version. A few plants and one creature."

"What's that sound?"

"A type of cricket, a local variety. Don't get too close to them, though. They have sharp teeth," warned Germann. Bohatch showed Karina an earlier bite on his forearm. "They eat the plants, but all animals are opportunists. They'll take meat any day of the week."

"Ooo, nasty," said Karina. "Then why have them in here?"

"The boss loves them, especially their sound. He finds their 'music' soothing," replied Germann. "I think he has a point." Karina listened for a moment. Yes, it had a certain something about it.

"What about the rats? Don't you have them in here too?"

"Rats? They're not indigenous to the planet, so no. Good for stew on Thursdays, though." Karina wrinkled her nose. "This way." Germann led Karina through a large clump of tall plants on the right. Veres had already gone ahead as soon as they'd arrived at the level, whereas Bohatch stood at the lift doors, guarding.

"Veres! Who is it?" Karina heard yet another voice ahead, stern, authoritative. This must've been the boss. Both herself and Germann walked into a small enclosure, a type of office area surrounded by tall, green plants. Veres was at a comms system, and another older man sat on a three-legged stool.

"Kotschky," replied Veres. The old man waved his hands in the air and shook his head, lipping 'I'm not here' while giggling.

"He's not here, he's... in the Northern Outlands, camping." The old man started giggling louder. "What? Yes, he has the breathing apparatus... no, he's not too old to go camping... What? He was meant to organise what? The pipes? Again? Oh, I see, well, sorry but he's not available at the moment..." Veres pressed the mute bottom on the comms system. "Hey, keep it down, boss." The old man tried to fight back his merriment as Veres put the comms back on. "Yes? Sorry, what? Oh, yes, well, yes... he is that." The laughter stopped and the old man gave a bemused look. "Well, I'll give him the message... yes, I'll inform you as soon as I know anything. Goodbye." Veres switched off the comms and noticed Germann and Karina.

"Well? What did he say?" asked the old man on the stool.

"You're a shithead," answered Veres.

"I know that. Now, can we move on? What have we got on the agenda today? Anything important?" The old man also spotted Germann and Karina. "Ah, a visitor!" The old man's eyes lit up. "Come in, come in!"

"This is Viranyi, our boss," whispered Germann.

"MTSG," said Karina to Viranyi with a half-baked salute. Well, he was the boss.

"What did she say?" he asked Veres.

"MTSG... remember? The salute?"

"Oh! Yes, I remember now. So..." He stared at Karina for a while. "So, I've heard you are a police officer, and not just any police officer."

"My name's..." started Karina.

"Yes, yes, Karina Reif, and the other's Borsodi. Yes, Veres has informed me already. Two police officers. And you're out of uniform? Well, that's against the rules... nice company suit... but... what the hell happened to you?" Viranyi pointed at Karina's implant. "Is that...?" Germann grabbed Karina's shoulders to pull her head down towards Viranyi to give him a closer look. Karina pushed back.

"Get off!" She fought Germann's grip and stood up.

"What is it?" asked Viranyi. "Is it an implant?"

"Yes."

"You have a computer fitted directly to the brain?"

"Tell me about it," she muttered.

"The things they do nowadays." Viranyi shook his head. "Does it hurt?" Karina had to think about that one. *No, it does not.* Speak for yourself.

"It has some ill effects," she replied. *Please state the 'ill effects' for further enhancement of processing and compatibility.* Well, for a start... *Unable to comply.*

"Anyway," asked the old man, ignoring her words, "how do you like the place so far? I'm sure Germann has already shown you around." Germann nodded. The nodding man. Definitely a 'yes' man.

"Well, I've seen the inside of one of your prisoner cells and the neutering of one of your men, so, yes, I've seen quite a bit. Haven't made up my mind yet as to how I feel about it."

"Ah. Sarcasm, wit. We're kind of lacking in those departments here," said Viranyi. Grabbing a long walking stick, he stood up from the stool. "What about this? My little personal paradise on this shitty planet," he said, sweeping the stick around to show the place off.

"It's nice, though I've just heard that the natives bite."

"Natives? Oh, the crickets. Ha. Yes, they do. Nothing serious, though. Nothing that won't stop me from keeping them here." He walked out of his 'office' and into the large area they'd come from. With the stick, he activated a large monitor from the floor near a wall of plants and it appeared, finally standing from hip to shoulder height. "You are our first visitors since AxiCorp left us to die. Some of us did." Karina heard shouts between Germann and Veres in the 'office'. "Don't mind them, a heated discussion keeps their brains from frying in this emptiness." Karina found herself nodding as Viranyi opened up a 3D map of the whole complex on the monitor. She'd already seen most of one level.

"This installation was a mining colony for almost thirty years, mostly mining vanadium and other minor metals. Then they ran out, and so did AxiCorp." He gave a dramatic pause. "They took all they could and left us here. No profit in picking up miners once the goods are gone. They're two a penny in the company." Karina looked at the map of the installation again. Comparing it to Gubacsi Dulu, it was much smaller, but it still had its offices, work dormitories and entertainment areas, as well as the mining areas lower down.

"I see you have all the facilities," said Karina.

"Yes, we do, well, we did, they're mostly redundant now. Those areas here, here and… here…" He pointed with his stick. "They are now extra turbines from some of the old mine lifts which have been refitted to create more energy for the colony. We had to become more self-sufficient fast, which came at a heavy price." He sighed. "There was one hell of a commotion when we had to close down the bar."

"I was hoping for a drink," said Karina. "Or maybe a bite to eat."

"Oh, of course, yes. How rude of us. I'll see to it straight away." Viranyi nodded over to Bohatch who still stood guard at the door. With a tut, Bohatch opened the lift and disappeared. Viranyi's stick tapped on Karina's shoulder. "I haven't seen… a police officer for a long time now."

"Really?" Karina tried to picture the people she'd seen so far, all mostly typical working overalls, casual clothes except for Bohatch in his body armour. No real uniforms. "Where are the uniforms? Every installation has them, no matter how small."

"First to go."

"To leave?"

"No, first to go. We had only one police officer, but he was a waste of space, so we had to let him go." Viranyi touched the top of the monitor with his stick and it dropped slowly back into the floor.

"Let him go? Where?"

"Outside."

"Is the planet habitable?" she asked, already knowing the answer.

"For the crickets and these plants, yes." He said nothing else.

"So you threw him out... to die?"

"We threw him out, yes. Whether he died or not, I cannot say. Schrödinger's cat, you know? If you don't open the box, you cannot really know."

"So you murdered him."

"Those were... difficult times, people were upset, angry at AxiCorp, at the system. He got in the way of change. There are always those who suffer due to change. It's taken a while to work it all out but all in all we're a friendly colony now. Quite happy, really." Viranyi started back to his 'office' as Bohatch came out of the lift with a flask of drink and a sandwich sealed in a transparent box. He waited for Bohatch to hand them over to Karina.

"What's the drink?" she asked.

"It's a type of tea we make from natural ingredients here in the colony," he said.

"And the water?"

"What about the water?" he asked, confused.

"Where is it from?"

"It's collected from the rain on the surface and filtered to purify. Where else would it be from? We don't get water shuttles coming in here. Except yours, but that's contaminated."

"Just asking. And what's in the sandwich?"

"You've got a lot of questions. I don't know, some kind of synthetic cheese, I think."

"Okay, thanks." At least it wasn't meat. And rain water. Excellent.

"Wow, are you always so fussy?" asked Bohatch.

"Only with what I put in my mouth." Whoops. That came out wrong. "I have to be careful with my diet." The men both nodded. Viranyi went back to his 'office' where things had gone a bit quieter and she followed him in. Bohatch went back to guard duty, while Germann and Veres had taken standing positions on opposite sides of the 'room', sending cold stares at each other every now and again. Karina drank and ate while the old man sat on his stool and watched. An audience. The drink was hot if nothing else, while the sandwich was cold, stale and hard. As she was shovelling in the last bite, the lift opened and she heard Bohatch 'outside'.

"What d'you want?" he said.

"I've heard about our visitors, I'd like to see them," said another voice, another man.

A thought entered her mind. Men. So far, all men. Okay, not so strange, seeing as it was a mining colony and miners were still mostly men, but back at Gubacsi, women were still a part of the work force. Where were the women? She'd ask later. Something was definitely not right about the situation — Borsodi's incident, for one. What had happened here?

"Boss!" shouted Bohatch.

"Let him in!" replied Viranyi. He spoke to Karina. "I forgot to mention. There's one uniform left. His name's Klemm, a state guy, lower management. Somehow he got left behind. If I were AxiCorp, I would've done the same." A short man in an AxiCorp uniform with the official state badge over his left breast pocket entered Viranyi's office.

"MTS…!" He started a salute and stopped abruptly, with what looked like both shock and disgust at seeing Karina.

"I… I was told there were two of them," said Klemm, straightening his uniform after finishing his salute. Karina sipped on her drink. Without taking his eyes off Karina, he spoke to Viranyi. Both Germann and Veres turned away. "I was told there were two female police officers."

"Where do you get your information from, Klemm?" asked Viranyi.

"You are meant to keep me informed of any happenings! I am the only official member of the state here!" steamed Klemm.

"Shut up, Klemm. The state has no authority in this colony anymore," said Germann.

"You...!" He pointed to Germann. "You will be the first... the second to feel the might of the state when they return." Germann looked slightly upset by that. Did this guy have clout, or was Germann not so tough?

"Put your finger down, Klemm, you could hurt someone with it," said Viranyi. "Yes, we have two visitors. One of them is with the Doc now, the other here, and yes, they are both police officers and yes, they are both female."

"What's with the female part?" asked Karina. There was a moment of silence and the conversation continued without her.

"Is the other one sick? Has she got the virus?" Klemm backed up a step, still eyeing Karina and noticing her head.

"No, they're both clear. The other had an... incident with Bolond. We had to deal with him," said Viranyi.

"Did he go for a walk?" asked Klemm.

"No, we need all the hands we can get nowadays. No more walks, Klemm... unless... you'd like to take a stroll? I'm sure we could use the extra oxygen."

"What's wrong with her head?" asked Klemm, ignoring the casual threat. He probably got them on a daily basis.

"It's an implant. And I can hear you, no need for the third person," said Karina. Veres gave a chuckle.

"He never knew how to speak to women," muttered Veres.

"Now who's using the third person?" she replied, which made smile.

"Why are they here? Are they here on recon for the state?" asked Klemm.

"Recon? No, they were forced to land here, well, crash-land here. This one is Karina Reif," said Viranyi. Klemm went white.

"Karina... Reif?"

"Yes. Any more questions? No? Good. Germann, could you please show Karina to her quarters, I'm sure she'd like a rest from her... tiring day." Germann nodded. "Karina, I hope you will find them better than your first here."

"Ha!" laughed Veres. "Stuff the corners with socks if you don't want to be a midnight snack." Karina gave back a smile.

"Oh, and I apologise for the behaviour of my colleague, Bolond. Your companion did not deserve such treatment from one of us. Not all of us are strong in spirit." Were there any women in the colony? Is that why this Viranyi was speaking like this? Nineteen years without a female in sight? Karina could only stand, think and wonder. Germann gestured to her to follow him, so she nodded a goodbye and walked out. As they left, she heard Viranyi cursing at Veres for putting Bolond and Juhasz on the detail.

011

GERMANN and Bohatch took Karina up a few levels in the lift and the doors opened to reveal yet another poorly lit, whiteish-walled corridor. "Most of us live on the level above this, but we've cleared you a special room for your stay down here." Stay. How long was she staying? Long enough to find someone to crack the code in the tablet? The tablet! Where was it?

"Where are my things?" asked Karina.

"Your things? What, like clothes?" asked Germann. "We didn't really find much in the shuttle. I don't remember anyone mentioning anything of consequence, unless that shaver we found is yours?"

"No, it isn't."

"Good. I'd rather not give it back, its blade is quite new," said Germann, stroking his smooth jaw. Get back on track. The tablet...

"I didn't really have time to pack my best, especially under the circumstances, but no, I didn't mean clothes. My essentials, like, my weapon, my tablet, my comms, those things," she replied, trying not to give any hint about what was important.

"Your weapon? I'll ask Viranyi about that. We try to keep weapons down to a minimum down here. As for anything else, Bohatch can escort you back to the shuttle if you'd like?" said Germann.

"Yeah, that would be good." Karina stopped. "How about now? Which way is it?" She pointed down a few corridors.

"Err, now isn't such a good time," he replied, looking at his personal comms. "How about later?" He stopped in front of a door, not waiting for a reply. "Here we are. Your room." He took out an entrance keycard from his pocket and swiped it over the lock. The door slowly swished open. "Mmm, I'll get Puskash to look at that for you. It's a little slow." A small light lit up and she saw a room, slightly larger but much cleaner than the cell.

"Okay. Then can I go to the shuttle later?" Germann nodded at her question. "Okay, well, thanks for the room." She stepped inside. An image flashed through her mind. Borsodi. "When can I see Borsodi?" For some unknown reason she had a need to see her, make sure she was alright. Sisters together? Was it a girl thing? In fact, how far could she trust anyone? These guys? Was the devil she came in with her best shot? What exactly was she doing here and what, if anything, did they want of her? Or Borsodi? The thousand lines of thought made her shiver.

"She's with the Doc at the moment, he's dealing with her condition. Perhaps you can see her later, too, though I really have no idea on that one," answered Germann. "Get some rest, that's the best thing for now. Tomorrow is another day." The door swished shut and Karina was left alone. There was a bed over in the middle of the left wall and she went straight for it, falling onto it and staring up at the small ceiling light.

They knew who she was, but how much did they know? Was she the instigator of the virus, or the holder of the cure? How much information had got to this desolate, forgotten colony? Had they seen the tablet and all it held? They for sure didn't seem to know much about brain implants, so maybe they didn't know anything about the vaccine, either. No way to know, only time would tell. These guys were... strange. But she didn't blame them. Being left for dead for nineteen years would do things to your mind. That Bolond guy would be an example of that, but then the way they implemented punishment seemed too clean cut, too blunt. No grey areas, just black and white. These guys were dangerous. They had lines, rules. She had to get that tablet before they realised what was on it. Maybe she was too late.

'Get some rest', the guy had said. Sleeping wasn't an option. Fifteen minutes staring up at the ceiling did nothing for her. The beep was a godsend. Was that you? *No, the comms in the room is beeping.* Thanks. Karina got up and looked around. By the door, a panel was flashing. She went over and pressed what she thought was the comms.

"Yes?"

"Hi, errm, my name's Puskash, I'm the tech guy for the colony," said thin voice over the comms.

"Hi, 'Puskash'. I've heard of you. What can I do for you? Have you come to fix the door?" She hadn't met this one yet but Germann had mentioned him.

"Er, no. What about the door?"

"It's slow to shut."

"Oh... right. Er, do you have a moment?" he asked.

"For what?" What did this stranger want? And that was the point. What?

"I heard you have an implant. I've never seen one before and I'd like to take a look at it," he said.

"That's a new line. Does it always work?" she asked.

"Excuse me? I... I don't understand. I... saw some preliminary work on prototypes before leaving Earth but I've never actually seen an implant up and running, so to speak," he said. This guy sounded honest enough. "Can I see it?"

"That depends," she said. Should she ask? "Are you any good at hacking?"

"Yes, why? Do you want to hack your own implant?"

"No, well…" *That would not be wise.* Oh, shut up, I'm just kidding. "Something else."

"Oh." There was a pause. "You're not talking about that tablet from your shuttle, are you?" Shit. He had the tablet.

"Err, yes?" What did this guy know?

"Oh, I cracked that hours ago. Wanna see what's on it? I can't make head nor tail of it, myself."

"Oh. Great. Erm… okay. Where are you?" Karina tried to open her locked door but a red light appeared. They'd locked her in. "Damn."

"I'm two levels up, Room 542. Take the lift at the end of the corridor."

"I can't get out. They've locked me in." At that, the door opened. Quickly.

"Anything else? I can set the lights to show you the way if you want?"

"Err, no, that's fine. Where were you again?"

"Room 542. I'll be waiting. Oh, I'm not armed, so don't worry, I'm 'armless," he said, giving a giggle.

"You're only after my mind, eh?" she asked.

"Excuse me? Oh, yeah, something like that."

What was there to lose? This Puskash guy seemed legit. And a bit… immature. Tech guy, through and through. Karina stepped back into the corridor and allowed her door to close behind her. Take the lift at the end of the corridor. Which end? The lights lit up, as promised.

012

KARINA followed the lights to the right, all lit up by Puskash, down to the end of the corridor. She heard a few squeaks as she passed one half-closed door and stopped to look inside, hearing movement in the darkness of the room: rats, tons of them. With that 'revelation', the lights in the corridor flashed. What was this? A power cut? They flashed again in the same sequence. Was it Puskash, could this Puskash see her? If so, was he helping her or was he impatient? *There are is no surveillance equipment.* Then how? *Unknown.*

At the end of the corridor was a beaten up metal door, most probably the lift, seeing as there was a panel next to it showing up and down arrows. She pressed the up button and a light flickered on… and then off. She tried again. The same thing, on, then off. Perhaps that's how it worked. She waited.

Four minutes and twenty-three seconds. What? *Waiting for the lift.* Oh, right. Is it coming? *Negative.* Then what? *Take the stairs.* Where are they? *Next to the lift?* Looking both left and right there was nothing, only walls, dirty, grimy walls. The dim lights didn't help. She looked back down the corridor she'd come down. Maybe the stairs were at the other end?

She didn't have time to take one step. Suddenly the closest door opened and Bohatch appeared. He was zipping up the front of his armour jacket when he looked straight at Karina without flinching and finished the action.

"It's not safe for you to be alone in the corridors. That's why we locked your door," he said. "How'd you get out?"

"Umm…"

"Puskash, huh? And what are you trying to do? Use the lift?"

"Umm…"

"Did Puskash tell you to use it? He doesn't know it's broken, hasn't worked in months. Doesn't leave his computers much, you see. Once when I went in his room, I found a layer of dust on him."

They stood there for a moment. The nearest light above flickered.

"He wanted to see me," said Karina. Bohatch blinked, the only action he'd done since zipping up.

"Okay. I'll take you to him." He waved for her to follow him down the corridor. She guessed to the stairs. "But before I do, d'ya fancy a drink?"

"Like what, that tea you gave me?" she asked.

"A drink drink, you know."

"You have some?" Alcohol would be good at this point. *Warning: check potency before consumption.* Who are you, my mother?

"Sure. How do you think we've survived for so long? Of course we have drink. It's not exactly company standard, but it sure beats the tea," said Bohatch.

"Okay." What else could she say? Bohatch led her all the way down the corridor and they took the stairs up for one floor. Entering the corridor she noticed it wasn't the same as any other she'd walked through. On the whitish walls was graffiti, mostly names but some murals and 'signatures'.

"Most of us live on this level, but it's usually empty now, everyone's out doing their duties. Here, this one's mine." He showed a card to the door and it swished open. The whiff of two-week-old used gym socks hit her. She was going to ask if there was any room service but that might've hurt his feelings. Taking another sniff she wondered if she should go in, for health reasons in the least. She watched him from outside going to a wall compartment and taking out a bottle from a selection and grabbing two glasses. He turned to see her still standing in the corridor. "I don't bite." He placed the glasses down and filled both with some brown liquid. "Okay. I'll put your mind at rest." If only. He got on his comms and typed. A beep came back. "There. Puskash knows you're here. He's waiting for you. Hang on." He typed some more. Another beep back. "And no, he doesn't want to join us. See? Anti-social." He gestured for her to come in and sit. She did and he slid over the glass to her side of the table. "Cheers." They both grabbed the glasses and Karina watched Bohatch take his first swig. He smacked his lips and nodded for her to try.

"Cheers." It smelt right. I tasted... unpleasant. "Ooo, what is it? I thought they banned petroleum products centuries ago?"

"Ha. Ha. One of the guys ferments this down on level 12. He uses wheat ration powder."

"That's evil stuff to eat, let alone drink."

"That's why he ferments it." Bohatch took another swig. "Thirty-five percent. Good enough for me."

"Yeah, but how much can your body take before it starts to rot from the inside out?" Karina gave it one more go. "That ration stuff is all synthetic." Her mind flashed to the water tanks, the shuttles, the crowds of people... she took another swig.

"Been drinking it for years, hasn't harmed me yet," said the guy whose room smelt like the Academy's gym's men's changing room — Karina wouldn't know what that smelt like, of course. He put his glass down and sat back, resting his clasped hands on the belly of his armour jacket. "So, you're the famous broad who wiped out millions of people. That's something."

"I didn't wipe them out. The virus did. I was merely... I just... fell over," she replied.

"What? We intercepted a message saying you were a mass-murderer and instigator of the virus."

"I had it in my top pocket. Someone shot me and I fell. It flew out of my pocket and some kid stepped on it."

"I'm sorry, what?"

"I had the virus, yes. But I was trying to get off Gubacsi Dulu. I... I... they wanted to kill me."

"Why did they want to kill you?" he asked.

"I knew..." Should she tell him? Did he know? As far as she could tell, no one in the mine colony knew. "I'd just had enough of all the corruption, I was trying to get out, but you know what they're like. Once in, always in."

"Yeah, you're right about that." Bohatch nodded in agreement. "Unless profits go down. Or you mutiny. Or both. Then you're out." He filled his glass with the bottle again and swallowed it in one gulp. "How come you had a virus in your pocket?" Yeah, how come she had a virus in her pocket? "It's not standard issue. Not something you can get off a shelf."

"I..." The drink wasn't helping. "There was this crazy scientist. I got involved in some investigation, I can't remember the details... I died, you know, and then this." She pointed to her implant. "Half my brain was shot out."

"Yuck." He stared at her for an embarrassingly long time, and then stood. "Well, you're here now. And Puskash is waiting. Would you like to hear some of my poetry?" Where could she run to? He must've spotted her instant reaction of dread. "Right, well, it's been nice. Shall we go?" With a swish of movement, they were both out in the corridor.

"And short," said Karina. "It was a short visit." Bohatch gave a quick nod and he climbed the stairs to the next level with Karina following.

"There you go," said Bohatch. "Third door on the right. Mind your step."

"Thanks," said Karina. "And thanks for the drink. It was… an experience." He tipped an imaginary hat and disappeared down the stairs.

"I'll be seeing you, Karina," he said.

073

ROOM 542. The door was half open and Karina saw a row of monitors and a ton of cables strewn across the floor. She slid open the door and in a small black swivel chair sat a thin man, balding, but with a long goatee and… goggles. He turned from the large monitor he was examining.

"Hello, come in!" He got up and showed her a seat close to his own. There was nothing else in the room except for a horseshoe of desks with monitors stacked on them from one wall to the other. And some empty sandwich containers strewn on the floor. He kicked a few under a desk. Each monitor was busy, numbers ran down them, across them, with pictures and graphs all flashing before her eyes. Karina cautiously stepped in and took the seat he'd offered. The guy immediately examined her head. "Oh wow, it's… pure… genius."

"If you say so."

"How did you get it? I mean, how was it attached? I mean…" He blushed. Typical info guy.

"Half my brains were blown out by a laser rifle and this crazy guy put it in my head and brought me back to life." Cut a short story shorter.

"Ah, Frankenstein's monster," said Puskash.

"More like G.D.'s monster."

"Mmm?" The guy was still analysing the outside shell of the implant. "Ooo, there it is."

"What?"

"A terminal, the interface connection." Here we go again. They only ever wanted her for her mind.

"It's not gonna do you much good. There's nothing in there except for a few kung fu tutorials and how to fly a water shuttle."

"Huh?" Puskash disappeared under one of the desks and reappeared with cables. Yes, here we go again. "May I?"

"Be my guest." Why not? Everyone else had. Puskash delicately connected the cables to the implant and sat back down, swinging over to one particular monitor while tapping away at his console.

"Wow, talk about 'access unlimited'. This entry file runs for miles," he whistled. "But not 'access all areas', there's a file here…" He tutted. "Anyway…" He was quiet for a while after that.

"How does it feel?" he asked.

"In what way?" In terms of weight, she felt nothing, in terms of thought, nothing. Sometimes she felt heat.

"I mean, the preliminary programs which ran the prototypes I saw on Earth were primitive. Sometimes the volunteer patients suffered from adverse effects such as dementia, epilepsy, bipolar incidents, depression, that kind of thing. Have you felt any such symptoms?"

"Not for a few minutes." He looked over to her and touched his goatee. "I talk to myself sometimes." Or did she? *The implant is part of you.* Then I do. *Biologically speaking, no.* Then I'm like a split personality. *Please specify 'personality'.* Crap, first you tell me you can't find my soul, and now you tell me you don't know what a personality is? Or maybe you can't find it? Do I have one? *Please specify 'personality'.* I hate you. *That is acceptable.* "For example now."

"What is it saying?" This guy was interested.

"That it doesn't know what a personality is. Maybe I don't have one," she joked. Puskash didn't laugh.

"I know a guy like that." He hit a few buttons and a ton of data flashed across the screen. "Wow, that's... oh. Who put this in? The implant, I mean, not the recipe for Goi cuon. I'll take that, by the way." He moved some data to a new folder.

"I said before. A crazy guy, by the name of G.D. Why?"

"You're lucky it works at all. He almost fried the main processor. Look." Karina looked closer at the screen. Numbers. And?

"Uh.huh?"

"Hang on." He hit a few more buttons. "What are you thinking about now?"

"Now? Well, nothing much. I was thinking about whether you had a beer or two. That Bohatch gave me some foul drink but..." A flash. Then another. Someone screaming. It was her. Another voice shouted 'yes' — it was G.D. Another couple of flashes and she was looking at a ceiling. G.D.'s face appeared and then it disappeared in a cloud of smoke as G.D. started swearing. A flash. And again. More screaming.

"Well? What did you see?"

Karina was back, sweating. "I don't really know."

"I accessed the earliest data since installation. How well did this 'GeeDee' do?"

"I think... from what I just experienced it looked like he had no idea what he was doing."

Puskash went over to another monitor and copied something over. "I can work on this, though I'll need some time. Mmm..."

"What can you work on?"

"A better connection. I wonder... if I try this..." Karina's head lit up. She felt stronger, more alive… then it stopped. "Oh. Damn. A firewall just went up. Did you do that?"

"Me?" What was the implant up to? Silence. "No. I have no idea how it all works, I'm just the host."

"Okay. Damn. Then this could take a while." Puskash went back to the first monitor and tapped away.

What did you do? *The bipedal Borsodi does not appear to be in the medical centre.* I'm sorry, what? What are you telling me? *I was able to peruse the mainframe before it connected completely. Its system is outdated and slow.* Uh-huh. It felt good. And? Hang on, you said 'I'. *A pronoun is needed. May 'I' proceed?* Affirmative. Silence. Of course, go ahead. I can't believe you can't take a little sarcasm. *In the time allowed, I was able to extract a certain amount of information. The bipedal Borsodi is not being kept in the medical centre but rather a secure area.* What? A secure area? *I was not able to find the location of the particular area.* Why? Not quick enough? *Affirmative.* So she's not sick? *There is no indication that she is neither sick nor healthy, merely inactive.* Inactive? Sleeping? *If sleeping includes being in an induced controlled unconscious state, then yes.* What's happening around here then? *Nothing is ever as it seems.* What's with the philosophical quotes? *I did not wish to alarm you. You and the bipedal Borsodi seem to be in danger.* Tell me something I don't know. *Hair grows at 0.44 mm per day, while yours averages a growth of only 0.21.* Really? Am I going bald?

"Mmm, looks like I'll have to get out my code cruncher again," muttered Puskash. "Oh, before I forget, your tablet." He reached under another desk and gave Karina the tablet. It had been cleaned and smelt of lavender.

"Oh, thanks." She swiped the screen open and there it was, every folder sitting on the desktop, waiting to be opened. One folder in particular stuck out from the rest, it had a strange name, 'Hab0159'. That had to be the one the implant had tried earlier. *Affirmative*. Good. She double clicked it and it opened, showing a document of the same name. Double clicking that, the read program opened it. Karina's heart beat through her chest. Was this really the vaccine? *Affirmative*. Come on, open, open, let's have a look…

"Yes, I opened that one as well," said Puskash. "Tried everything to break the language. You need the specific ciphers that created it in order to read it." He was right. The document opened to show gobbledygook. This was the vaccine, all right… *Affirmative*. But Hadidi had written it in a code or language only he knew. "I've placed the document on another computer. Would you like me to run a decryption program on it? There might be a chance it'll work."

"Yes, please. It's part of my… research," she said.

"Your research? Then why don't you have the cipher?" he asked.

"This one was… erm… written by my co-researcher. Unfortunately he was… taken by the virus." And what a lie. A whooper. Might even work.

"I see. Okay." Puskash hit a button. "Done. We'll see what…" There were two shadows hanging over them. Puskash turned his chair. "Hi, guys." It was Juhasz and… Bolond.

"What's she doing here? She's meant to be in her quarters," said Juhasz. Bolond was silent but looked uneasy.

"I was just running some diagnostics on her implant, nothing serious, I…"

"Does Viranyi know about this?" asked Juhasz.

"Well, I… err…" Puskash stuttered over his words and shrunk back in his chair, away from Karina.

"Thought so. Miss Reif, could you please allow us to

accompany you back to your room. For your safety," stated Juhasz.

"What, like the safety you gave my companion earlier?" scowled Karina.

"Things are different now. I... I'm truly sorry about what happened. My friend here... he can be a bit... impulsive at times."

"I wouldn't call it 'impulsive', I'd call it obscene, inhumane and a ton of other things. 'Impulsive' isn't one of them," said Karina, trying to put some anger in there. Puskash was already taking off the cables from her implant.

"Yes, yes, you are quite correct. If it makes you feel any better, Puskash can also accompany you back," said Juhasz.

"What? That's meant to make me feel safer?"

"I'll... I'll take her back. Alone," offered Puskash. Juhasz stood for a moment and thought.

"Okay, but I'm gonna have to tell Viranyi about this." He nodded and they both stood on either side of the open door, Bolond taking a little more time to move.

"Okay, yes, okay. Sorry." Puskash took Karina, now holding the tablet, by her left elbow and moved her past the two men who watched them leave. At the end of the corridor, Puskash let her go. "You need to get back to your room now. For your own safety."

"My safety. So, it's not because I'm a prisoner here?" Puskash said nothing. "Okay." She held the tablet with both hands. "Thanks for this."

"No, no, thank you. I have enough to work on for weeks, perhaps months now."

Karina nodded a goodbye and descended the stairs to her level and room.

074

LYING on the bed. Eyes wide open. Silence. Again. A low murmur of the motors in the airducts above the ceiling reminded her of the installation at Gubacsi, especially G.D.'s hideout. Claustrophic, too. And cold, even with the body warmer. A lapse of concentration brought a flash of Pukanszky's last grin, the one before she shot him in the head, through her mind, along with the feeling of intense rage and intrusion. Had he violated her in any way? There was no real way to find out. *Data insufficient.* Yeah, well, she had been dead for a while before the implant. And maybe even a little dead before her death. *There are minute traces of certain chemicals which might lead one to believe this was the case, though this fact is circumstantial as they could also come from other sources, such as natural or artificial.* What could she say to that? All she knew was Borsodi had been violated, if it were true, and she was going through some mental torment by herself and in her own way. Where was she? *A partial map of the installation is available.* Really? *Through a process of elimination, her location can be found.* Then what are we waiting for? "Shit," she said. She was a prisoner in her own 'guest' room. 'For her own safety.'

She got up and tried the door. Perhaps placing her hand on the door lock panel would work? Nothing. The red appeared again. At least it registered she existed. She felt… vulnerable in this 'safety'. When were they going to allow her out? When they came for her? And what did they want? What were they going to do to her? A succession of images sprung to mind, none of them good. The best was that they knew they had 'Karina Reif', the infamous 'terrorist' who set off the virus, or at least that's the story they must've heard. Maybe they were going to use her as a bargaining tool to bring AxiCorp back. She tried her hand again, a little harder, and in the shape of a fist. No go.

"How the hell can I open this?" Can you help? *My help would cause you great pain.* Oh, really? You can open this? *Affirmative, though it would cause you great pain.* How much pain? *Enough to make you think whether it is wise to try such a course of action.* How. Much. Pain? *Have you ever put wet fingers in an unearthed live electric socket?* No, that's crazy. *Then I recommend you do not try such a course of action.* Would it open the door? *Affirmative.* Would it kill me? *Negative... recalculating...* What? *...the chances of dying are... slim.* Slim, thanks. Then? *This is my final warning.* Shut up and do it. *Place the right side of your head against the door lock.* What, are you going to listen to the cogs turning in the lock? *I will send an electric pulse through the lock, thus short circuiting the apparatus and opening the door.* 'I' again huh? Silence. Oh. Right. What's the best way to get through an electric shock? *To go around it.* Funny. Karina placed her head against the lock, as ordered. Now what? "Ahh!!"

Pulling herself off the floor, she spat out the phlegm which had collected in her mouth due to the spasm of pain. Looking up, the door was open. It worked. *Affirmative.* Why didn't you tell me it was going to hurt that much? *I see that experiencing is believing for you.* You should know. *Unfortunately, yes, it has been the case so far.* Oh, shut up and help me get up. Energy was moved around her enhancement suit to allow her to stand easier, then it evened back out across her body. Stepping out, the corridor was empty. "You would've thought they'd posted a guard. Okay, which way?" *Eliminating known areas.*

Unknown areas found. Turn left, use the stairs on the right. Go down three flights and open the second door on the left. Then... Hang on, hang on. Remember who you're dealing with here. A pattern emerged in front of her eyes, stencilled on the walls. A large red line appeared, moving down the corridor to the left. That's neat. *Follow the line.* Thank you. Could you make it yellow? *Would you like breadcrumbs to retrace your steps?* What are you on? *I am in. In your head.* What side of the bed did you wake up on this morning? *I did not wake up this morning, I do not sleep.* Shame. The line changed to yellow.

After twenty minutes walking, going down half-lit corridors and stairs, and through doors while not meeting a single soul, Karina wondered where she was going. *You are approaching an unknown area.* Where are we? *On level twenty-one.* How many levels are there? *Four hundred and fifty-five.* Well, it is a mining colony. A door appeared at the end of the corridor under the shadow of the light halfway down the corridor. She tried the handle but it wouldn't budge. There was a keypad on the wall. Great. She tried a few numbers and of course, nothing happened. Now what? Another shock to short circuit the lock? *I strongly advice against such a course of action.* What else am I going to do? While she was deciding on whether to try it again, the handle suddenly turned without a touch, making Karina jump backwards. She ran down the corridor and hid in an alcove a few metres away. She heard the door creak open and someone stepping out. The light from beyond the door filled the corridor. Then the steps disappeared back inside and the light diminished. Looking back into the corridor, she saw the door swinging shut. She took her only chance and dove for the door. Her left hand slid between the door and frame. Without her enhancement suit, the weight of the door would've crushed her hand. *Good catch.* Thank you. She slipped her right hand into the gap and pushed open the door. Careful not to make any more noise, she slid her body through like some handicapped snake and let the door close behind her. The light in the room was blinding but after a few seconds her eyes acclimatised. The first thing she saw in the pure white-walled room was a pair of eyes. A child's eyes.

"Are you okay?" it asked. Karina pushed herself away and saw the eyes belonged to a boy, probably six or seven years old. He was dressed in a nice white overall and had short, trimmed hair. He looked familiar somehow, and also quite concerned. "Who did that to you?" He was pointing at her head, the implant. Always the implant.

"It's... yes, it doesn't hurt." Karina was a little shocked. Not only had it been a few years since she'd seen a child, she was definitely not expecting to see one here. And yet... how? Maybe there were families here, maybe... maybe that's where the women were, if at all! That would explain a lot. They were down here, safe, looking after their children while the men worked, keeping the colony alive.

"All right, then." The boy smiled and walked away. Karina quickly got off the floor and followed him. He was heading for another room.

"Hey, where are...?" Another boy poked his head into the room. He had the same face as the first. What? How could that be? The first boy turned to her — two faces, exactly the same. Twins? Now that was something. "Where are your parents? Your mother?" asked Karina.

"Sorry? What?" asked the second boy.

"Your parents. Father, mother? Where are they? I'd like to meet them." She smiled to try and reassure them, or perhaps herself, that everything was alright.

"What are those?" asked another child, walking into the room. The child's hair was longer than the others... the child looked at Karina. It was a girl. She looked like... the two boys, though more feminine.

"What's going on in there?" asked a male voice. Karina heard his footsteps. "Who are you talking to?" Karina suddenly got the urge to run, a streak of fear shot through her spine, and she headed for the door, opened it and sprinted down the corridor, hearing the door close after her. Had the man seen her? Who was it? And why was she running? She hadn't done anything wrong, except for escaping from her room... cell. And where was her room? *Follow the yellow line.*

It took half the time to get back, and lucky she didn't meet anyone on the way. She got to her room and found the door still open. Covered in sweat from fear and exhaustion, she slumped into the room and pressed to close the door. It stayed open.

"Oh, come on! What's the problem!?" *It is short circuited.* So it won't close? *I do not recommend this next course of action.* What course of action? What do you mean...? That...? *Affirmative. Apologises.* Now not under her own control, her body stood up and her head was placed against the door lock. No, not again! The sharp jolt of pain threw her to the floor.

075

THE two warm, sweaty, slabs of meat wrapped around her face that were Bohatch's hands were enough to bring her around.

"She's back!" said Bohatch.

"We can see that," said Germann. "What the hell happened here?" Puskash was there, too, sitting on the floor and messing with some cables at the door.

"It looks like she tried to short circuit the door lock with an electric pulse from her implant. It didn't work, though, just fried the door shut," said Puskash, checking out the circuitry. "That was one big pulse, though, this cable's shot. I'll have to strip it all down and replace it."

"Don't bother, we'll just give her another room," stated Germann. "Miss Reif? Karina?" He bent down to her.

"Yeah?" She pulled Bohatch's hands off her face and sat up.

"Why did you try to open the door?" asked Germann.

"I wanted to go for a walk but the door was locked. Why?" she asked. They thought she'd failed to open the door. Good job, too. If they knew what she'd seen... what had she seen? Oh yeah, kids. Children.

"Why, she asks," Germann said to the others. "For your safety," he said to Karina.

"So everyone keeps telling me. From what?" This 'safety' thing was all a ruse, no one wanted her out to see what secrets they had.

"Not all of us at the colony are as civilised as those you have met so far," said Germann. "Some are like Bolond, base and susceptible to their desires. Others are worse." She imagined there could be, with almost two decades stuck in a mine, but this was probably just a lie to keep her from doing what she'd already done, snooping around, finding out what was going on. She'd keep quiet about what she knew. No telling, not yet. "How are you feeling?"

"How do you think? Bohatch, have you got any more of that rain water?" she asked. Electric shocks made her throat as dry as Gubacsi's desert plains.

"Sure," he said, passing a hip flask. "If you don't mind catching me cooties."

She opened the flask and wiped the edge with her sleeve before gulping down some. Cool, fresh. "Thanks." She passed it back and asked for a hand up, which he obliged. "See, no cooties."

"Your companion Borsodi is recovering well. I've come over to ask if you'd like to go and see her?" said Germann.

"Is she still with the doctor?" asked Karina. Her implant had told her this wasn't the case. It would be interesting to find out exactly where she was.

"Yes, he's running a few more tests, but she seems fine now. The... incident took its toll on her," he replied.

"It would. Assault isn't pleasant, especially that kind." They all dropped their heads. "Well? Can we go?" she asked.

"Of course, of course," replied Germann. Both himself and Bohatch allowed her to pass and enter the corridor. Puskash stayed behind, on his behind, examining the door lock.

"Forget it, Puskash. Go and check out the room next

door, see if it's in working order," ordered Germann.

"Yeah, okay, it's just..." Puskash continued to examine the door lock.

"What is it?" asked Germann.

"Nu... nothing. Okay, I'll have a look at next door." He picked up his tools and headed to the next room. Karina then followed Germann to the medical facility. She already knew where it was, thanks to the implant, so she pretended she had no idea where they were going. Bohatch stayed a few steps behind. For safety? Hers?

The two guys took Karina in a different direction, down more corridors, some stairs. They turned one corner and the smell of gas instantly hit them. Smoke moved over them and filled their sight.

"What the hell...!" screamed Bohatch. Germann held Karina back while Bohatch went ahead down the corridor. He came back a few moments later. "Those damn... Mexicans... we can't go this way. One of the pipes burst." Karina could hear Germann swearing under his breath. She saw his mental gears working all across his face. What was he thinking?

"Okay, change of plan. Maybe you can go and see her tomorrow," said Germann.

"We could go through C-section and across to the medical..." Bohatch stopped talking. Karina caught a look from Germann towards Bohatch.

"Yeah, Germann. We could go through C-section and across to the medical," repeated Karina. She smiled at Germann. She already knew there were 'unknown' areas for her of the installation. *C-section is not on the map retrieved.* You see? The man paused for a moment.

"Okay." He rushed off in another direction. What was this 'C-section'? Why didn't Germann want her to go in that direction? What were they hiding?

Apparently not much. Just a lot more corridors, corners and doors, with the occasional hissing pipe overhead and blinking light. Sometimes a cold wind blew down on them from above.

Then she saw something as they sped by an intersection.

"What's over there?" she asked, stopping. She'd seen a guard on a door. She almost hadn't seen him, all dressed in black. But he had a laser rifle, at the ready.

"Important stuff," said Germann. "That's why we have a guard on the door." They hurried her down another corridor which looked like all the others.

"What's so important? And why the guard?" Germann gave her a look of distaste. "Your boss said you're a friendly colony, and that everyone is happy here." He sighed and stopped, putting his hands up in surrender.

"You can still get the odd one or two who drink too much after a hard day's work. It only takes one drunken idiot to destroy the party, you see. Can we go on now?" Karina shrugged, but before he'd taken another step, her next question came out.

"So what's behind the door?" she asked. Germann stopped and Bohatch bumped into the both of them.

"If you must know, the energy system for the colony, some turbines. If anyone messes with them, it'll take months to repair and by that time things could get a bit hairy around here." Karina nodded. "We're here," he said, pointing to a door with a black caduceus sign spray-painted on it, a staff entwined with two serpents and a set of wings at the top. "The medical facility." He opened the door. "After you." Karina hesitantly stepped inside. What would she find?

076

THE scene in front brought back memories for Karina of her old doctor's surgery back on Earth. There wasn't much to see, white walls — nothing new in this place, a few perspex-fronted cupboards full of medicine and supplies, a couple of empty treatment tables and an assortment of medical machines and equipment. The only person in the room was an old, tall bald man in a white coat looking over some consoles on a far wall.

"Doc! I've brought the other visitor," said Germann, taking a seat by a table as soon as he came in. Once the Doc turned to them, Bohatch nodded a greeting and left the room, probably going back to the corridor.

"Hello Germann," said the Doc. He stood a few metres away and examined Karina. "Ah, the other visitor, a Miss Karina Reif, I presume? Doctor Golen at your service." He stepped forwards and held out a hand for her to shake. She hesitated but finally gave hers. His hand was hot, strong and a bit sweaty. On the last down shake, the Doc slowly pulled her closer to see her implant. "Ah, yes. I have read so much about these. Interesting." The interest spanned some seconds as he continued to hold her hand. He then let her go and offered her a seat in gesture. Karina sat next to Germann, away from the doctor.

"She's come to see…" began Germann.

"Yes, her companion, I'm sure she has," said the Doc. He went over to a different console and examined some numbers as they scrolled across the screen.

"So, she'd like to see..." said Germann.

"Yes, yes, our visitor? She's not here," said the Doc.

"What?" said Karina. Germann sat back in his chair and didn't say another word.

"Your friend and colleague," stated the Doc, "is suffering from post-traumatic stress disorder. I have her sedated. She is in another more secure part of the installation for her own safety." So that's why her implant couldn't find Borsodi in the medical facility. Maybe she should relax a little and trust more, cut down on her conspiracy theories. Maybe she was over-reacting. It was difficult to be among all these men and not think of being under some kind of threat, but maybe there was nothing sinister about the whole situation. Maybe they were, mostly, good guys trying to survive, trying to move forwards. In fact, what were they trying to do here? But the children, what about them? "So, unfortunately, due to this, you can only see and speak to her through this console," informed the Doc. He stared at Karina too long for her to feel at ease. She stood up and crossed the room to sit down at the console and pressed to open up the comms. A screen showed Borsodi, her head lying on a pillow, facing up.

"Borsodi?" asked Karina. The girl turned her head on the pillow to face the camera.

"Yeah? Karina?"

"Yeah, it's me." These were the first words she'd heard from the girl since they'd been boarded by those guys. "How are you?" What else could she say? Such a feeble question.

"I'm getting treatment. For what I don't know, but... the Doc says I'm stable and I... should get rest."

"Apparently you've..." The Doc's hand pressed the

sound of the comms off and hovered over Karina.

"Please don't tell her what she has, it might take her back into a state of shock, which in her condition could be fatal." The Doc looked straight into Karina's eyes. He was serious. She pushed his hand off the comms.

"Karina? What did you say? You... you got cut off," asked Borsodi.

"The comms equipment here isn't what it should be. Apparently you've got a few more days in there, so you should get some rest while you can, just as the doctor ordered," she said, taking the Doc's words into account. He looked happy.

"That's all I can do in here," she said. "There's no cable, no radio, no nothing."

"There's not much out here, either, unless you like repeats of *Fraggle Rock* with all the characters played by forty-plus-year-old men." No laugh, just an empty stare into the camera. The Doc hovered over her again. What was his problem? He anxiously made a 'timeout' sign like some NFL coach six points down with only seconds on the clock. "I've gotta go, but I'll be seeing you."

"Okay." Borsodi turned her head back to looking up from her pillow. Karina turned off the comms.

"What the hell is wrong with her?"

"As I said, she is suffering from post-traumatic stress disorder, which can bring on many bouts of silence and retrospection. Reliving the past."

"I know what retrospection is." This guy was the most irritating person she'd met... in days. How was he a doctor? Where was his bedside manner?

"She can seem a little... short, but it is to be expected," said the Doc.

"When will she be allowed out?" she asked. The Doc shook his head.

"You make it sound like she's a prisoner," he retorted. "I assure you, she is getting the best treatment available."

"That doesn't change the fact that you're holding her in a 'secure' place." The Doc said nothing to that. "When will she be healthy enough to be able to…" What was Borsodi trying to do with her? Trying to get her back to Headquarters, that's what. "…complete our journey?" And how? Their shuttle was kaput. Actually, no one had mentioned anything about the state of their water shuttle, except that they weren't unloading its cargo.

"Soon, soon."

"How soon is soon? Is that soon as in 'I'd better go and clean the cockpit out for tomorrow' or soon as in 'I can read a good book or two while I wait'?" Was there an engineer here in the colony? That was the question.

"I'd choose the latter, if I were you," replied the Doc. He gave a quick smile. "I'm sorry but I'm a little busy at the moment. There was a burst pipe not some minutes ago and I must go and examine some injuries."

"Yeah, we passed by that area," said Germann.

"How bad is it this time?" asked the Doc.

"I'd take your mask," replied Germann.

And with that, they all left together, the Doc with his medical bag and a mask, and Germann and Karina, with Bohatch in tow. The journey back to her room was longer going back. Germann added a few more detours to miss out the burst gas pipe and also the strange guarded door, Karina guessed to stem her curiosity. When they got back, Puskash was still working on the lock of her new room, the one next door to her old one. Without a word, Germann and Bohatch smiled at Karina and left her to sit in her new room as Puskash sat there, twiddling with some buttons and cables.

017

HE wasn't moving. Puskash had been there hours, scratching his head, playing with his goggles, pressing buttons, pulling on cables and making fizzing noises accompanied by electric smoke and quiet little swear words. Karina wanted to rest. She needed to rest. Or at least be left alone for a little time. They always wanted her to do something or go somewhere. A little time to think would be nice. Her implant beeped.

Your physical vehicle will be shut down in 2.34 hours to restore healthy levels. What? Another shutdown? Why? Do you mean 'sleep'? *Negative.* So you mean you will shut down? *Negative.* Then what? *Your physical vehicle will be shut down in 2.34 hours.* Again? *This will be the first time since initial boot up.* What are you going on about? *You have insufficient fat storage in your physical vehicle. It will shut down in 2.34 hours for a period undetermined.* Oh, so you won't shut down… but my body will? *You must gain some adipose tissue soon.* What? *You need to eat.* So I have to eat? *Affirmative.* But I have been eating. A little. *Your stress levels have recently increased dramatically due to your recent circumstances and the excess fat in your gluteus maximus was utilised to produce the stimuli hormones and chemicals to allow an adequate service of your physical vehicle at this time. The latest drain on your body has created a critical situation.* What drain? *The door lock.* Oh. So hang on, you took fat from my bottom and turned it into a stress reliever? *Affirmative. Unfortunately, the fat-to-muscle ratio of your lower body is now at a level which is dangerous to your health and so there are two alternatives, shut down or eat more adipose* tissue. Fat? *Affirmative.* So, you're asking me to eat more fatty foods? *Affirmative.* Okay. So I have a skinny arse now? *Affirmative.* Oh. She felt her behind. Yes, it was true. The last time it was that size, she was running in the half gravity playground with the other kids in her community. At least you didn't take anything from my boobs. *Insufficient fat content was found in that area.* I'm sorry, what? *Insufficient fat content was found in the area of your mammalian protuberances.* What are you saying? What! Has anyone told you that you're a piece of shit? *Running at 86% efficiency.* Karina smacked the side of her head. And now? *Such an action is not recommended.* Up yours. So what now? *Adipose tissue is needed.* Fat. *Affirmative.* "Have you got a sandwich?" asked Karina to Puskash. He lifted his goggles off his face one more time.

"Eh? Yeah, sure." He slid over to a rucksack and put his hand in. A moment later he passed her one of the sealed sandwiches she'd received earlier. They tasted of nothing and had nothing in them, no nutritional value and definitely no fat content.

"No, not one of these. Something with a lot of… grease, you know, something dripping. Something with fat. A big, juicy whopper of a sandwich."

"Uh-huh. Tricky. But I could try and order one."

"Okay." Puskash nodded and started sending a message on his comms. Is that good? *This is the beginning of a…* Beautiful friendship? *Do not interrupt. Of an acceptable diet which under the circumstances you find yourself in will lead your physical vehicle to a healthier state.* You really are a piece of shit.

"Done." Puskash had pressed a few buttons on his comms. He stared at her. For a long time. And then blinked. "I know what you did," he said.

"What's that, then?" asked Karina. What had she done?

"With the door lock in the other room."

"Yeah? I tried to open it. And? I feel like a prisoner," she said. No reply to that. "What else was I meant to do?" He shrugged.

"No, you didn't try to open it. You had short-circuited it twice. Once to open, then again to close, but the second time was too much for you physically," stated Puskash.

"So I just heard."

"Sorry?"

"Nothing. Just got a status report from 'you-know-who'," she said, pointing to her head.

"Oh." He continued working. So he knew. What was he going to do? Tell on her? What were they doing there? What was her plan, or even theirs? This place was getting more and more difficult to handle. Could she trust anyone here? Back on Gubacsi Dulu, she had to take care and pay attention on a daily basis, but she never got the feeling that she was ever in any real danger, even as a woman among a majority of men. But here it was different. She felt... exposed. And now this guy knew she'd sneaked out.

"It's not safe to do that," he said. "Firstly, you could blow the implant, secondly, you could hurt yourself physically, and thirdly..." He stopped taking.

"What?"

"What has Viranyi told you?" asked Puskash. He put his tools down and turned, sitting cross-legged at the still open door.

"Ooo, that sounds sinister," she smiled. Yeah, it did. What the hell was going on here? And what about those kids?

"No, really. And where did you go?" What should she tell him? He seemed a nice guy, but then, so did G.D., though he was much stranger than this guy.

"Oh, not far. I just needed some air," she lied. And he knew it.

"I guess Viranyi told you we're getting along swell in this little colony of ours," he said, ignoring her last remark.

"Well, yeah, he did." Why? Weren't they?

"There's a bit more to it than that. I've got to say that…" He stopped talking and restarted his work on the doorlock, and Karina heard why. Footsteps. Germann was back, though with Juhasz in tow this time.

"Did you miss me?" asked Karina. Germann gave her a tired grin. She guessed not.

"Viranyi would like to have a word," he said. And that's all he said as he stood there at the open door. Juhasz stood behind him as any dutiful little guard would do.

"Okay." Karina pushed herself off the side of the bed she'd been sitting on and accompanied her entourage to Viranyi, leaving Puskash to swear at the door lock as more smoke appeared from the circuitry.

"I'll send the sandwich over to you," said Puskash. She lipped a 'thank you'. Walking between Germann and Juhasz, she felt like a sandwich.

"Haven't you sorted that yet?" asked Germann to Puskash as they were leaving.

"No! Ahh!" Puskash sucked on a burnt finger.

078

VIRANYI'S 'office' was the same as before, plants all in a row, creating a green wall surrounding them. Karina thought they were in some potted, preened hedge forest with out-of-place furniture and a mismatched collection of costumes for the animals sitting around, sipping their drinks. Her sandwich had arrived, as Puskash promised, and low-and-behold, it was greasy and twice as thick as the one he'd offered before. By the time she'd finished there was a small puddle of remains on the floor, which many of the men present studied intently.

"I've asked you to come here because I'd like to know your plans," said Viranyi. Finally, someone had asked. What was next? They'd 'landed' on what they thought was an uninhabited planet with an out-of-use facility because their turbines had failed and found themselves in a colony of... miners. And Karina was now alone, with Borsodi ill somewhere after being assaulted by one of them.

"Plans? Well, we were trying to get to Headquarters, so I guess that's my plan," replied Karina. Germann and Veres were also there, sitting, with Juhasz standing at the 'door'.

"Uh-huh." Viranyi scratched his head while reading through something on a portable console. "And if I may ask, why where you going there with a shuttle full of contaminated water?"

"It was the only transport available." That was true. "We weren't thinking of spreading the virus or anything sinister like that." One thought had crossed her mind a few times, and that was of adding the vaccine to the water. If they could produce some once she'd found out its components.

"You could have jettisoned the whole consignment in space, then everyone would have been safe," he said.

"Yeah, of course. But we didn't have much time to think. As soon as we'd started, our turbines stopped working." She watched Viranyi look at his console.

"Yes, so it seems from the shuttle's log." He placed the console down and crossed his fingers together in his lap, rocking his chair back and forth. "Listen. I know you have plans to leave this place as soon as possible..." Germann chuckled at that. Viranyi scalded him. "But you see, if that were possible, we would have done it ourselves a long time ago."

"So, there's no way off this planet?" she asked. He'd made a good point. If that were true, then what? What was she going to do? Out there in habitable space, thousands, perhaps millions, she didn't know, were dying from a virus of which she alone had the vaccine. Encoded but all the same she had it. How was she going to get it to them? Hang on. Why did she care? Was it really her responsibility alone to get it to them? Maybe Headquarters had already started a search. Maybe others would come and try to find them. The military, AxiCorp. "Don't you have anything? We saw tug shuttles, they helped us land."

"Only good for use within the atmosphere. No, we have nothing."

"Can't you get a message out? Call Headquarters?" she asked. Why was it getting more claustrophobic in here?

"Our poor communications off-planet are incoming only due to an unfortunate incident when AxiCorp left," replied Viranyi. "The main antenna was damaged and we have no one knowledgeable in that area. Puskash tried but it's not his particular field of expertise."

"Perhaps I can look at it," said Karina. Can you fix an

antenna? *It is possible with the right equipment and materials.*

"Surface conditions are harsh at best. It would be nigh on impossible with the tools we have at hand. No, there is no way to contact the outside universe unless we can gain orbit, which we can't."

"So where does that leave me and Borsodi? Are you saying we're stuck here?"

"Unless a miracle happens, unfortunately, yes."

"What miracle?" They usually came at a price.

"That we get another visitor, though the chances of that are indeed slim to none."

"So this is it? We're all stuck on this planet, in this colony?" Her lips felt greasy and she was about to wipe her mouth with her sleeve when Viranyi offered her a handkerchief, which she used.

"Yes. This has been the reality for us for almost twenty years. As we are a colony of mostly men…"

"I haven't seen a single woman since I got here," Karina interrupted.

"There are some in the colony, perhaps you will meet them some time," nodded Viranyi.

"That would be nice," she said.

"Yes. As this colony is mainly populated by the male of the species, we have yet to see how having you here will affect our situation."

"Well, as you said, you do have women here, so how is the situation going to change?" she asked. "If at all?"

"That is what we have yet to find out. In the meantime, I would like to say that you are welcome here, to stay, though it would be nice if you could work while you are here. Along with Puskash on the tech side of things, for instance."

"What, because I have an implant?"

"Precisely."

"So, you're saying that he can use me, rather than I can help him?" They only wanted her mind. *Technically, it is not yours*. Shut up.

"Erm, you could see it that way, but I'd rather say that you would not only be helping him but also the whole colony for years to come by creating a more efficient and energy-effective system."

What could she say? No? Get me off this planet? I don't care how, just do it? "Whatever. At least I'll have something to do."

"Yes."

"I can be a productive member of the community, unless a miracle appears," said Karina, trying to show some enthusiasm in her situation, when in fact, she knew it was bullshit. What were they up to?

"Exactly. Thank you for your understanding, and I'm sorry for this... inconvenience," ended Viranyi.

"Inconvience? Being stuck on a planet with nowhere else to go? Well, yes, it is. But as you said, what can we do about it?" Viranyi nodded and relaxed in his chair.

"I'll take you back to your quarters," said Germann. Karina held her hand out for Viranyi, which was slightly greasy. He gave it a soft shake, taking back his handkerchief, and with a smile she followed Germann out, with Juhasz taking the rear. Which would soon be bigger after a few more sandwiches like that.

079

JUST as they were turning a corner close to Karina's room, Germann stopped. "Oh hell, I forgot." He tapped his forehead, though it looked like playacting. "The Doc wants to give you a health check, you know, before you start settling in and all."

"Okay..." That sounded like a genuine thing, but the way Germann gave it, Karina still felt a bit weary of it. "What kind of health check?"

"How would I know? He just said you should come over and let him do a few checks," said Germann. "Juhasz, can you take Karina back to the Doc?" He checked his comms for something.

"Okay, no problem." Juhasz touched Karina on the shoulder. "Follow me," he said. Karina was surprised she was left alone with just one guy, and this one in particular.

"I've got a few things to do, you'll be fine," said Germann. He must've noticed her concern.

But there was nothing to worry about. A few corridors later they were both at the Doc's. Juhasz knocked on the door and it swished open.

"Ah! Come in, come in," said the Doc. Juhasz stayed outside while Karina went in. "Please, take a seat." What was this? Another chair? Another room, corridor, walk around a mine? A life of walking around and sitting down? That's all she ever did here. Life in this place was starting to get so repetitive. The Doc sat opposite her and smiled.

"So… Doc, what's up? What's the deal? They said you wanted to give me a health check?" she asked. Although he was looking straight at her, the man was lost somewhere, his eyes glazed over.

"Mmm? Health check? Oh, oh yes! Of course." He got up and went over to a counter, putting on a pair of sterile white rubber gloves and collecting a few tools of the trade: syringes, wipes, swabs. Typical brainhead, away in their own thoughts. "Here we are." He sat down again and wheeled over a shelf to place all his equipment down. First he wrapped a blood pressure monitor around Karina's upper arm and watched the numbers going up. "Ah, not so good, but you'll live."

"Thanks, Doc." He then stuck an empty syringe into her other arm and took a vial of blood.

"Cut down on greasy food and get more rest."

"Sure." Did you get that? No greasy food. *More Adipose tissue is needed to raise body levels to a healthy standard.* He gave her a wipe and made her hold it in her arm to help it clot, and took a swab from the side, and back, of her mouth. "What's that for?"

"Oh, many tests." The Doc collected the samples and moved back over to the counter. In the silence, Karina could hear something. Scrapping.

"What's that?"

"Mmm?" The man was away again.

"That noise." She heard it again. "That."

"Oh, that." He looked over at her and smiled. "I'm a doctor, a man of intelligence and learning. Some have said I'm a genius." Love yourself much? "Are you aware of how long we have been 'held' here in this facility?" he asked.

"Yeah, almost two decades," she replied. "Well,

everyone tells me that, anyway."

"That is a long time dealing with mainly fractures, burns, cuts, boils and piles. A better man would go crazy."

"A better man?"

"Yes, well, thankfully I have a few specialisations to involve my mind," he said. She heard a few more scrapping noises, but now she realised from where. Behind a door on the back wall.

"Specialisations? What kind?" What kind of doctor was he? Was he connected to what she'd seen before, the kids? She'd heard an adult male voice, but it wasn't the Doc's. Were there other medical staff people here? "Are you alone here in the mine? Do you have any helpers?"

"Please. AxiCorp could hardly pay my salary, let alone another," he laughed. "Would you like to see my menagerie?" What was with this place? Everyone had their own personal zoo?

"Err, why not?" She wasn't sure what kind of animals she was about to see. He was a doctor. Experiments, tests, lab rats, that kind of thing. Were there horrors behind the door?

"Oh, do not worry, I don't have any 'live' specimens. Well, not many." She grew more concerned. What was she going to see? Dead animals in jars? She'd heard scrapping, so there had to be something alive. "Come this way." He placed his comms over the door lock and entered the next room and disappeared. His hand appeared and waved her through. What could she do but follow. The room was dimly lit, as usual, but the room was covered with machines.

"What are these?"

"DNA scanners, replicators and manipulators. One of my specialities was as a geneticist. Not to be confused with geneticism, of course. Pseudo-science was never my thing," said the Doc, looking over a few machines and their screens. "These are my only luxury. Viranyi allowed me to keep them, seeing as I am solely responsible for the health and welfare of those imprisoned here. Puskash wasn't allowed to gut them, that monster." He stroked the nearest machine. He certainly loved his speciality. DNA machines. Karina's hair stood up on the back of her neck and she didn't know why.

"So, this is like... a hobby?" she asked.

"Hobby? It is my life work, my form of expression, my art!" He recomposed himself by stretching and twisting his neck. "Please." He gestured her to come closer to one machine. "Can you see that?" She looked at a screen full of numbers and letters, with a spiral diagram showing certain patterns and colours. *DNA sequences.* Thanks. No need to help.

"Okay, DNA. That's DNA. So what am I looking at?" she asked.

"Human DNA." He pressed a few buttons and the screen shivered, showing more numbers and letters. "Now primate. Chimpanzee." As far as she remembered, there were still chimpanzees – in captivity, of course. She looked, the screen now shared the data together.

"Sorry, but my eyes can't really tell the difference," she blurted out. She was no doctor. *Analysing data.*

"And that's what earlier geneticists said. Not much difference at all. 1.2% difference between the human and chimpanzee genome. Other apes and primates, however, can have as much as 7% difference," stated the Doc, moving over to another machine.

"So, yeah, we're just hairless monkeys, eh? Some of us are more hairless than others," she said, smiling. Both herself and the Doc had a common problem.

"Quite, but the difference is the key."

"The key?"

"Look at this," said the Doc. "What can you see?" He'd set up another screen comparing human DNA with another.

"Oh, I can actually see a difference here," she said.

"I hope so. That's banana DNA," he laughed. "There is a 60% compatibility, would you believe? Life has similar basic building blocks, whether it's flora or fauna."

"Is this the key? And what door does it open?" she asked. The Doc tutted and moved to yet another machine.

"And this one?" he asked.

"Uh-huh." This comparison was strange, with much more data than the second DNA sequence or the human had. "And what is this? Something from Radnoti X?"

"No. I do have more data from indigenous species of this planet, but that only strengthens my argument rather than shining more light, so to speak. No, this is the apple genome, which has more genes than any other living known species in the universe, twice as much as the human. Do you know your bible?" asked the Doc.

"Who's religious nowadays? Not really, but I know about the apple, who doesn't?"

"The apple came from the Tree of Knowledge of Good and Evil, if you believe a book written by a group of scribes thousands of years ago," said the Doc. What was he going on about? "Perhaps the apple was the source of all knowledge, DNA knowledge, and that is why God told Adam and Eve never to consume the fruit, as it was the holder of the secret to knowledge and life." The Doc's eyes grew larger as he stared into space. This guy was as crazy as they all were. "Anyway, I digress. Here." He showed yet another machine.

"How many machines have you got?" she asked.

"Many." This comparison was close, but not as close as the chimpanzee.

"What is it? A pineapple?"

"Pig. 84% compatibility. But…!" His finger went up. "This is merely data. Here is my work." On the other side of the room were more machines, similar though slightly different, with mechanical moving parts added to the screens.

"More machines?"

"Please. Indulge me. It is not often that I have a new pair of eyes to look over my work. The others are either uninterested or do not see the relevance," he moaned. "This is a chance for me to see whether I have made a break through or am I shouting on deaf ears?"

"Okay." Karina went over to the machine and he motioned her to look at the screen. There were many sets of DNA sequences, one of them being human. "What am I looking at now?"

"Oh. Yes, a moment." The Doc opened up the screen on a neighbouring machine. The two screens were copies, except for the batch numbers of the sequences and a few numbers which meant nothing to Karina.

"They're about the same. Except for the titles?" she said.

"Some of them are exactly the same!" He shouted like it was some eureka moment.

"Okay, so from the screens I can't see what the point is," said Karina. *Analysing data.* Thanks, but you've got nothing, right. *Affirmative. However, a hypothesis is emerging.* And? *It has yet to appear.* How shit are you? *Running at 83% efficiency.* Useless.

"On the left screen are the original DNA sequences of

the human genome and eight other primate genomes, including most importantly, the chimpanzee and the bonobo, being from the genus pan, as opposed to human which is homo." Percentages appeared as to how similar the eight were to the human. The two pan members had extremely close percentages. "On the right is my work. Look closely at the top two next to the human genus."

The top three are identical. I can see that. "They're identical."

"Yes!" The Doc made a little jump. "It took almost a decade of shooting in the dark to realise which, but after that it was purely putting in the tedious work of how and how much," he smiled.

"Very nice," said Karina. "So what did you find out?"

"That the genus homo was created by a mixture of the pan and sus," smiled the Doc.

"What?"

"We're part chimpanzee, part pig," he said. This guy was completely insane.

"If that were true, that would explain a lot of things," said Karina, "but come on, that's stretching science just a little, eh?"

"Stretching? The answer is right here!" He lost his smile. "Unfortunately, when one can of worms closes, another opens, if you excuse my French."

"French?"

"The big questions now are how, why… and who?" said the Doc. He had that glazed look again.

"Who? Why who? Aren't you saying that chimps interbred with pigs, or vice versa?" Biologically impossible, for sure. And she'd been with a few pigs before, but really? Chimps together with pigs?

"Mmm? What? Oh no, no. Perhaps there were some perverse chimpanzees who had their way with pigs or hogs, though this wouldn't match their tribal societal group rules, I'm sure. Homo sapiens are known to perform in such activities, though chimpanzees have more ethnical sense." A truer word had never been spoken.

"So then what?" *Experimentation.* What? How? Why? And... who? *Those are the exact questions which the learned individual has mentioned.* Oh yeah.

"Over 7 million years ago, 'man' was created."

"Hang on, hang on, do you mean 'God' created man?" asked Karina. "And what about... what about the Neanderthals, and all those other homo genus, all those links in our 'family tree'?" Where was this all coming from? *The database.* You? *Where else?* You are getting cocky. Don't I even have my own knowledge? *There are some remnants of memory which...* Oh shut up.

"I have researched all known 'links' in the 'family tree' as you say, and they are merely prototypes, failed models of the homo genus, the ultimate example being homo sapiens. Us." He said it with a big smile. Enough of the smiles, this man was insane.

"But then... why? And... who, if not God?"

"Go back through history, back to the first seeds of civilisation on Earth. Temples, stone circles, pyramids, all somehow connected across the globe, all pointing to and mirroring star constellations from those times. There can only be one real answer," stated the Doc. "It's simple. We were bred by another species much stronger, more technologically advanced than us. For what reason, who knows? Food? Cannon fodder? Subjugation? The reason is lost in time, but the footsteps are there in the DNA. I believe we were slaves. And to make sure we stayed that way, our DNA was changed slightly from one race to another across Earth, perhaps giving us physical traits more acceptable to our surrounding environments, whether hot or cold. We were also taught different languages so as not to be able to communicate with each other to work together and topple our masters."

"What? How can that be true?"

"The DNA doesn't lie." He said that way too seriously.

"Then what?"

"Perhaps our masters left or just died, leaving Earth to us. It didn't take us long to mess it up."

"That..." She didn't know what to say to all this. "That is just..." Karina suddenly heard another sound. Distant. Lasers?

"Oh dear," said the Doc. To be honest, he didn't sound too worried.

020

"CODE 20!" shouted Juhasz, poking his head in from the corridor.

"Oh, that is a bother," said the Doc. Both Karina and the Doc walked back into the main room and he locked the laboratory door slowly and carefully, checking the seal around the door frame. "Really, a sewage backup? Now? I could have sworn I'd heard some gunfire," he said.

"That's a Code 12, Doc! Yes, gunfire! Two levels down!" screamed Juhasz. "I'll have to get both of you to a higher level for safety!" The comms on the Doc's wall rang out, accompanied by a small flashing red light. He went over to speak.

"Doc here! Please state your emergency!"

"Casualties on levels 10, 11 and 12, Doc! We need you to get down here right now!" Karina thought she recognised the voice, probably Bohatch, maybe not.

"Okay, let me get some armour on and I'll be right there." The Doc shuffled off to a cupboard. "Juhasz, please escort Miss Reif to the higher levels."

"Okay, Doc. Just make sure you keep your helmet on this time!" said Juhasz. "I'm not good at stitches!"

"And don't I know about it," replied the Doc. "Off you go now." The laser fire was becoming more frequent. As Karina and Juhasz left, the Doc jogged off down the corridor.

"This way!" Juhasz moved in the opposite direction. Karina followed. Again!

Moving up a level, the laser fire abruptly stopped.

"What's going on?" asked Karina. "Who's fighting who?"

"Oh, just a little… disagreement. It happens sometimes," said Juhasz.

Suddenly the laser fire started up again, but this time much closer and just up ahead from them.

"Shit!" Juhasz spun around and grabbed Karina, flinging her to the side with a swish and a bang. The next thing she knew, everything went dark. It felt like she was in a box. With Juhasz.

"What the…? What are you…?"

"Shhh! Quiet… we're in a wall closet. It'll be safe here until the danger passes." Karina couldn't believe it. How could the place be even more claustrophobic than it already was? By being in a closet.

"Do you come here often?" she asked. No answer.

The laser fire was regular now, though further away. They stayed there for quite some time. Just as they thought everything had quietened down, it started up again. The silence and smell were killing. What did Juhasz use as soap? She'd hold her nose if she could've moved her hand to her face. The discomfort was too much for Karina so she broke first.

"So, I've, err, just heard a really strange theory from the Doc," said Karina. Maybe this would help to break the unease she felt in the closet with Juhasz between distant laser shots.

"Tell me about it," said Juhasz.

"Well, he thinks…"

"No, don't, I know already. He told us all years ago. Real nuts."

"Oh." More unease. "Do you have any 'theories' or beliefs? Being stuck in a mine for years, you're sure to think about things." She'd found the source of the smell. It wasn't Juhasz, specifically. "Such as washing your socks on a weekly basis?"

"Socks? No, not that. Me? Thinking? Don't do that much thinking."

"Oh, I can't believe that," she said. *Sarcasm never dies.* Didn't I tell you to shut up? A few laser shots quietened the conversation for a while. They were close. It must've been some 'disagreement'.

"But I was always infatuated with the Moon," said Juhasz in an excited voice, making her jump and hit her head on the roof of the closet. Laser fire flew right down the corridor. Karina could see the beams.

"The Moon? Oh, you mean Earth's Moon," said Karina.

"Yeah, the Moon. Is there another one?" he asked.

"Quite a few, yeah." She saw this wasn't helping the conversation. "So, it's... the Moon. What's so special about it?"

"Well..." Another laser beam shot passed them, but this time two more whizzed by from the opposite direction. "Don't you think it's slightly strange that a large object such as the Moon orbits the Earth? A large object in relation to the Earth, this is."

"It's smaller than the Earth, that's all that's needed, no?" she asked. They were all crazy. Every last one of them.

"Well, it's rather large as a moon for a planet, it's more like a daughter planet or a sister planet which controls the tides, the gravitational pull, the electromagnetism of its other 'half', and saves Earth from a multitude of meteors rather like a shield, spinning around, taking the hits and keeping us on the ground."

"Uh-huh, really? I never thought about it." Was there really something in what he was saying? Or had his brain turned to space dust through isolation.

"And that's the point." More laser shots went by from the opposite direction than the first. "It's so taken for granted, the Moon. Everything that it does, everything it does to help us live on Earth. It's like it was somehow... designed."

"What?" First she'd listened to the Doc, humanity was 'created' by some other superior species as a slave, and now the Moon was 'designed' to protect both Earth and humanity? These guys had been down this hole for way too long.

Suddenly the door to the closet opened and Karina gave out a yelp. It was Bohatch.

"Juhasz! What the hell are you doing in this closet with Miss Reif?" He was quite irate.

"Not what you'd like to be doing," accused Juhasz as he stepped out. Bohatch gave him a shoulder bump and Juhasz lost his balance a little.

"I'm sorry about this, Miss Reif," said Bohatch. "We had a little... incident below and it kinda got out of hand. It's sorted now. And I'm so happy you're alright." He gave his hand and Karina took it. His pull was strong and secure, and he held on for a few seconds longer than he should've, making her feel slightly uncomfortable. "I'll escort you to your room. Juhasz! Go help the others deal with the mess down below!"

"Okay, okay."

"After you," said Bohatch to Karina.

"Which way?" Karina stood there, smiling. Whichever way was fine with her. She had no choice.

"Oh, right. This way." Bohatch went first.

021

KARINA lay on her bed again. How long had she been laying there? *Six hours, thirty two minutes and...* Too long. Why couldn't she sleep? *You do not need to, it is an unnecessary procedure.* But it would be nice, it was something she used to enjoy, to be shut off from the world, to... *Would you like me to shut down for a preset time?* Oh yes, please. *How long would you like to sleep?* Forever. *That is not an advisable measure of time. Your biological vehicle would expire before then.* A few hours? *Affirmative. Shutting down in three, two...*

There was a knock at the door. *Countdown aborted.*

"Who is it?"

"It's me, Puskash! Viranyi would like you to come and help me with the mainframe! We had a bit of a problem yesterday and he was wondering if you could help," he said, shouting through the door.

"You mean my implant can help," she retorted. The door slid open.

"Yeah." The goggles were on.

"Is it safe for me to travel the corridors without a guard?" she asked. He looked sideways down both ends of the corridor.

"Err, yeah, I guess," he said. That filled Karina with confidence. She got up off the bed and followed Puskash out into the corridor, with him closing her door. The way to his little tech control room which stored the mainframe for the colony's system wasn't long and was completely uneventful, except that

Puskash checked every corner and corridor before allowing her to move on. He was jumpy, to say the least. By the time they got there, he was anxious. There was also a strange noise coming from inside her head.

What are you doing? *Calculating.* What? *How much processing capacity is available for the mainframe's processes.* And? *This will be... informative.* What does that mean? *The requirements needed are beyond the capability of the motherboard.* Oh. Is that all? It's never stopped you before. She came back and saw Puskash was sitting there, more disturbed than he was in the corridors.

"What's the problem, Puskash?" she asked. They sat down and he started shaking his legs in nervousness.

"Look, I've got to tell you this while I can."

"What? I tell you, I've heard and seen a lot so far. Like, what the hell was all that laser fire about?"

"Karina, you need to leave," said Puskash.

"I've only just got here. Fine." She moved to stand up.

"No, I mean 'here', like the colony."

"Ha! That would be nice, but I'm stuck here, we're all stuck here," said Karina. "As Viranyi said you've been doing your best to keep this place going until help arrives."

"Help won't arrive. Why would it? They've taken us off their maps. No one is coming," he said. "I don't know what Viranyi told you, but it's for sure he didn't tell you the truth."

"Which is?" asked Karina. He hesitated for a while, shuffling his feet and rubbing his hands together nervously, but he finally opened up.

"There was a strike, some disagreement about wage cuts and all hell broke loose in the lower sections of the colony. AxiCorp chose to leave, this place wasn't deemed profitable anymore, anyway. They were going to cut and run a few months later. That's how much we know now."

"I know all that."

"Did Viranyi tell you what happened after AxiCorp left?"

"Yeah, he said there was a problem but you were all able to settle your differences."

"No. We're at war."

"What? With who?"

"The lower levels. Well, it's kind of a stalemate at the moment, things have quietened down due to…"

"Due to what?"

"Survival. We have some things which they need, ie. the mainframe, energy, while they have some things we need."

"Such as?" she asked. He was reluctant to tell her.

"Your companion wasn't… assaulted."

"What? Of course she was. There was even a guy who got punished for it."

"Staged, for your benefit. What do you think we've been doing with our free time all these years? There are a lot of film buffs down here, and there's even have a drama club three times a week, down on level ten. And besides, do you really think they're going to hurt a healthy sperm donor?"

"A what?"

"Haven't you noticed?" What did she need to notice now? The obvious? Go for that one.

"I'm not stupid. You don't have many women, huh? So, sperm donors, what's that all about? Without women, that's useless."

"We don't have ANY women, well, WE don't." He scrunched up his lips like he'd let the cat out of the bag and then regretted it.

"What, hang on. The side you're fighting does?"

"Yeah. Bingo. A few. They took them during the chaos when AxiCorp left. They're prisoners down there, to use however they please."

"That's... that's horrific!" Karina didn't know how to feel about that.

"Yeah, it is."

"And you've all been here for years." This place had degenerated back centuries of social reform in just a few decades, when women were objects to be looked at, owned and used.

"Yeah, just imagine. Decades, without anyone coming to help or get us off this planet." Was he annoyed about the treatment of the women, or that he was stuck on this planet? She couldn't tell.

"So...?"

"So those in charge realised pretty quickly that the only way to survive was for the two warring factions to work together."

"What do you mean...? Oh, no. What? Okay, hang on. You're at war with the lower levels and you keep them alive with your power up here because... they supply you with women?"

"No! Not that! No! We're not barbarians! Not like the lower levels!" Puskash's face said it all, his features all squashed together in disgust.

"So what do you need women for...? The kids?" That made Puskash freeze.

"You've seen them?" He was shocked.

"Yes, I have."

"Oh yeah." He thought for a moment. "Yeah, that time you 'went for a walk'. Yeah, well, those kids are the successes."

"What the hell is going on here?" Why was she the one to always find out about something like this. First, it was the water, now it's... 'experiments'?

"Test tube babies. Or the closest thing to it. The Doc's speciality before being stationed here was vitro fertilization, but he was reprimanded for taking his work a little too far. Thankfully he did because if he hadn't, we wouldn't have the kids."

"So, you're making babies?"

"Yeah, kind of. They're our future."

"That's... that's unethical." For want of a better word. "What you're doing was banned over a century ago across the whole of society. Even China."

"We're our own society now. They abandoned us. So we abandoned their ethics. And then you arrived!"

"Two women." Karina wondered how they could fit right in.

"Well, one healthy living woman and you... a woman with a computer implant in her head." She always got the charmers.

"Yeah, 'cause I'm not a complete woman anymore."

"Yeah... no... I mean... you're just as precious as your companion, her as... what she is, and you as... what you are." Well put, nothing actually said.

"A monster."

"Yeah... no! Hell...!"

"Keep talking. What's changed?"

"Now we have... a woman," he said.

"Uh-huh." Biology lesson number one. "So you're going to use Borsodi's eggs from her ovary to help produce more kids?"

"Are using."

"Already?!" They were fast to take advantage of the situation.

"Yeah, the Doc drugged her as soon as you arrived. That's why she's in that state, not because of any stress disorder."

"Why didn't you just drug me? It would've saved a lot of time and trouble?" She wouldn't have needed to listen to this, for one.

"We tried. We found out the implant doesn't work well while its host is unconscious," he replied.

"Great. Okay, so because you now have Borsodi…"

"… we no longer have any need of the eggs supplied by the lower levels. Apparently most of them were becoming less and less, and more and more difficult to fertilize, too, seeing as the women below are getting older."

"So what now?" This was all a bit too much at one sitting.

"We win the war. We cut off their supply of power and let them die."

"Great. Congratulations. You murder I don't know how many people and enslave Borsodi like some chicken."

"And you." What? What about her?

"Me? You're going to take my eggs?" Enhancement suit? I may need to kick ass. *Enhancement suit running at minimal levels. Ass-kicking is a 'no go' area.* Great.

"No, we're going to replace our mainframe with your implant." *Not possible without the biological vehicle.* "It's much more powerful and more efficient. It'll run the colony for decades, maybe even a century or so."

"To do what?"

"Whatever Viranyi wants it to do."

"But my implant just said that's not possible without me." Karina gave him a smug grin. They just didn't know, did they?

"Simple. The Doc keeps your body alive while the implant runs the colony's systems."

"Wha... what happens when I die?" This... this was cheating! *With the correct medication and treatment, this is possible.*

"That's in the distant future."

"Why are you telling me all this? Why? Why are you dropping all this... shit on me now? Or at all!"

"Because I want to help you escape." Karina looked him dead in the eye. He was serious, or at least that's what she could see.

"What? Why? You've got us. We're defenceless. There's no way to escape," she said.

"I have my reasons." He turned to the console. And that was it? 'I have my reasons'? She needed more.

"What is it? It can't be power, or money. It has to be revenge? Is it revenge?"

"No."

"There has to be a reason." And what could that be? If it wasn't power, money or revenge, it had to be... love?

"Yes. I can't let them shut the system down on the lower levels."

"Why?" The one question that can break a conversation. They sat in silence for some minutes. He turned to Karina and took a large breath.

"They have my daughter." Blood. Yep, blood. The

strongest reason of all.

"Your daughter?" She thought it would've been a lover. "Why is your daughter here at all?"

"This contract, it was meant to be a six-monther, a stop-gap before my big chance on Earth. My wife was handling the deal, and she sent my daughter over for a few weeks to see me. Unfortunately, the trouble began right after she arrived." Puskash turned back, but he held something out to her, the tablet.

"That... is just unlucky. Hey, isn't that mine?" she asked. She moved to grab it but Puskash gripped it with both hands.

"Yeah, sorry, I took it from your quarters last time I was there. This... is your ticket out of here," he said. What did he mean? Did he know about the vaccine? "I can plug this into the system instead of your implant and the colony will run as usual... well, for as long as it's needed to fool the others and get out."

"But I need the tablet, I need the data on it," she pleaded. He was going to use her only hope of survival to escape? Without that, there was no reason to escape. She might as well stay in this place and rot, connected to the mainframe.

"Oh, the data? Hang on." He plugged in the tablet to the mainframe and swiftly connected Karina's implant with a cable. She felt a sharp stab of heat rushing through her head. "There, you've got it all. I've added my decryption program so that it can continue to work on the code there."

"What, all of it?" *Affirmative. Decryption program has recommenced.* Can you break the code? *We can but try.* Another quote? *Arthur Conan Doyle.* Whatever.

"Yep, all of it. Now can I use the tablet to help you escape this hell hole?" he asked. Why not?

"Sure, but what about you? Won't they realise you cheated them? Won't they punish you for this?"

"I'm coming with you. And anyway, I'm the only tech guy they have here. If anything goes wrong, I'll make up some cock-and-bull story about how you escaped and how I struggled to keep the colony going before being able to reconnect the mainframe. The thing's old but it still works. For now." Puskash pressed a few buttons. "Yeah, if my calculations are correct, once I plug this in, we have just over five minutes to get to the shuttle bay before anyone notices."

"And what use is that? The water shuttle we came in on is shot. All the turbines are gone. Viranyi said there's nothing to fly out in."

"Something else Viranyi didn't tell you the complete truth about, eh?" he said.

"What's that?"

"We have shuttles."

"Yeah, tugs. What use are they?" she asked.

"No, shuttles, for people. We have two."

"What?! So why haven't you just left the colony if you have ships?" These people were utterly crazy.

"This mainframe is built from their computer systems. And Viranyi didn't strip them of their turbines, considering they were miniscule compared to the lift turbines in the mine, which he used for creating extra energy. They are, however, dead electronically." Puskash gave her a smile.

"So what are you thinking? They're dead. Unless you think this thing can help." She pointed to her implant.

"Give me a few minutes and I can link your implant to a shuttle, and then you'll be gone, off this planet, away from this... horror." He made a gesture with his arm to show how they'd leave — how old was this guy?

"And what do you get out of it? Your daughter? How?"

"Ah. Yes. Well, I'm going to need your patience with that one."

"What do you mean?" Give the bait, then mention the catch. Always a catch.

"I will have to attach your implant to the system in order to help me locate and take back my daughter from the lower levels." He had it all planned. Did he have a life? Guess not.

"Okay, okay, every time you open your mouth this is all getting to be a bit more complicated and dangerous."

"Yeah. I'm sorry. But we're not living in a democracy here. But thankfully there's help."

"Help? So it's not just you?" What, more people?

"No. There are others."

"How many?"

"Enough."

"Enough for what?"

"Enough to get my daughter, get us off the planet and maybe even get some kind of life going again, together, me and her, somewhere else." He took off the cable from her implant.

"What about Borsodi?" she asked.

"Ah."

"What do you mean 'ah'?"

"I checked your water shuttle's systems and logs," he said.

"And? What about it?" There was more? Hadn't she heard enough today?

"Where did she say she was taking you?" he asked.

"What do you mean? Headquarters, of course. We're police officers. Where else would we go?" This wasn't the first time she'd been asked this since they arrived.

"That's not what I found." He flicked on a console and showed the coordinates.

"Where's that?" She didn't recognise the numbers. Not unusual, but every cop knew where Headquarters was, and that wasn't the place. "That isn't Headquarters. Headquarters is on Mars."

"This? I have no idea. The mainframe has a star chart which includes only the extent of AxiCorp's business ventures. This is out of that area."

"So, she was taking me to another destination, and an unknown one at that?" she asked.

"Yeah. How well do you know her?"

"She was a fellow student at the Academy."

"Looks like she lied to you."

"I should go and ask her," said Karina.

"Yeah, but she was going to send you there, wherever it is. So, why is she important to you? Why would you care about her fate?" Puskash brought up a star chart on a monitor which showed the coordinates to be in the middle of emptiness.

"Because she's a fellow human being? And a woman? And she knows what's in that place," said Karina, pointing at the star chart. Puskash sighed.

"Okay. I can add her to the plan if you want."

"Of course I want! No one deserves to be used like some experimental lab rat. So she lied about our destination, so what? Not a good enough reason to leave her here with… you. You're all crazy! This is… unbelievable, all of it. How could you do this? Why?"

"Needs must." He tapped his chin with a finger. "Okay, I'll have a think, try and get her out, too. But no one's going to be happy about it." He placed the tablet on a desk and stood up. "I'll need some time to set things up but Viranyi wants you up and running ASAP. He's ordered the Doc to come over tomorrow and discuss the finer details of your connection."

"Finer details?" What did that mean?

"Yeah, erm, how to connect you up, well, your implant and how to keep your body from just withering away."

"Oh, that's nice. Thanks. So all I am is just a brain to you guys," said Karina. Makes a change.

"Well, not your brain to be exact..."

"Thanks for the flattery." She sighed and wondered how she was going to survive this. What were her chances this time? Did she have to die? "Just... no more surprises, okay?"

"Okay. I know this is a lot to take in all at once but there's really no other way to go about this. After all this time sitting in this damn mine, every second counts." He tried to give her a reassuring smile but came out a bit creepy.

"Yeah, well, you could've gone about it a bit better, maybe even shortened it. Something like... 'Sorry, but we're using your companion, who lied to you about where she was taking you, as an egg factory in order to gain independence and win a war that's been on for decades so that we can take over the colony and live a decent life through the use of vitro fertilization while living under the rule of a hierarchical system. Let me help you escape this abomination, this closed, maniacal society while I gain back my daughter'." Puskash gave a short laugh and nodded.

"Sorry, yeah, that might've worked, too. I'll take you back to your quarters for now, but be prepared for anything. I'll unlock your door, too, that'll make things easier for you."

"Thanks."

"But stay inside until I send more instructions." Karina nodded. For safety.

022

KARINA and Puskash were about the leave when they heard footsteps outside.

"Puskash! Are you in!" shouted someone Karina didn't recognise. "Of course you're in, where else would you be?" said the man in a quieter voice.

"Who is that?" whispered Karina.

"It's Klemm."

"Who?"

"Yeah, exactly. The company guy." Puskash shook his head in dismay.

"Oh." Karina remembered the guy from when she'd met Viranyi. Uniform, slightly below average height, shiny badge. Puskash hit a button and the door opened. Klemm walked in and was about to salute when he saw Karina. He lost his balance slightly and grabbed onto the nearest desk. Standing up straight, he checked his uniform and cleared his throat.

"Ah, the visitor, Miss... Miss Reif, isn't it?" asked Klemm. What was it that Veres had said about him? Can't talk to women.

"Yeah. Visitor, I don't know, prisoner probably would be a better description," she replied.

"It is a matter of perspective," he replied. "It is for your own safety."

"As everyone here keeps telling me," she said. "Over and over again."

"What do you want?" asked Puskash. He was now sitting with his arms and legs crossed.

"The lights in my room don't work… again," he said. "I need you to check the system, make sure it's not on this end."

"Again? Already?" he asked. What did he mean already? Was this a recurring thing? Did Puskash expect them to not work at a future time?

"What's going on?" whispered Karina.

"Oh, erm, someone keeps messing with Klemm's lights. They usually do it only once a month, but it happened quite recently," said Puskash, whispering back. Klemm didn't seem to mind, though he'd heard their little conversation.

"Yes! And when I find out who's doing it, I'll report them to the state!" shouted Klemm. His face went red. Who's a little Hitler, then?

"Okay, I'll deal with your lights. Comms?" Klemm nodded and passed over his personal comms on his wrist and Puskash read some data off it. "Right. By the time you get back to your room, they'll be back on, all right?"

"Thank you," he said. He turned to Karina. "And how are you enjoying your stay at our colony?" Was he joking?

"Well, it's been quite 'captivating' so far, what with a cell full of rats, my new locked quarters and absolutely no privacy because everyone wants to speak to me or take me somewhere all the time."

"Well, Miss Reif, you are a rare commodity in this colony. Not only are you new to this place, and therefore a new pair of ears to listen to the sad, pathetic stories of these primitive men, you are also… a woman," said Klemm.

"Am I? I thought I was just an implant," she retorted.

"I'm sure for the likes of Puskash and his ilk you are that." Puskash snorted and Klemm gave him a stare. "But believe me, there are many here who would treasure you as a woman. And that is why you are being protected," said Klemm.

"I can protect myself," said Karina, showing off her moves with her enhancement suit. It wasn't working well... *Minimal levels...* so the fighting moves she showed with her hands — moves she knew in theory — but not practise — due to the download back on Gubacsi Dulu — were slow and clumsy.

"I'm sure you can," smirked Klemm. "However, I think you should thank us for keeping your door locked."

"Thank you," she said sarcastically.

"Humph." He heard it.

"Do you need anything else?" asked Puskash.

"Errr, no," replied Klemm.

"Then you can escort Karina back to her room, can't you?" Klemm stood for a moment, staring at Puskash. He bowed slightly as though he was a lord.

"It would be a pleasure," he replied.

"I hope not too much of one," muttered Karina to Puskash. He gave her a tiny smile and turned back to his monitors, replacing his goggles.

023

ANOTHER two hours on her bed staring at the flaky white ceiling under the dim light and there was a knock at her door. Couldn't they leave her alone, just for a moment? And to think of it, no, it wasn't a knock, more a 'collapse'. She got up and put her ear to the door. Was that mumbling she could hear? And then singing? Someone was drunk. Which meant one thing. Alcohol, more of it. She opened the door and Veres dropped his head into her room, connecting solidly with the floor.

"Greetings! 'Tis the merry warbler of Radnoti X!" smiled Veres.

"Have you got some alcohol?" she asked. That he'd had some was obvious. He lifted up a bottle, dirty, the label almost unreadable. "What is it?" This wasn't Bohatch's gut rot.

"Pálinka. Lasted years. One swig is usually enough to sooth the savage breast but tonight…" He waved the bottle in the air, it was almost finished. Karina grabbed it from him and gave it a closer look. It was ancient, the only number of the year left was the first, and that was '1'.

"Tonight? I didn't even know it was night. How can you tell?"

"It's always night, tell me different. It is dark, this is the case." He waved his empty hand in the air. "This is as it is, as nature dictates, and so, given the circumstances, the darkness, as it is, will always remain one and the same. Therefore…!" He halted in his lyrical lecture. Karina gave the bottle a sniff. Strong stuff.

"Therefore?"

"Therefore!" he gestured from the floor with his hand for her to take a sip of the bottle. So she did. Fire! Flames shot down her throat. *Warning. Toxins detected.* "If the darkness prevails, we can be sure that, in similar circumstances, it will always prevail!" His lips stuck together so he fought hard to separate them, then continued. "Consequently... it is always night." He belched, long and hard.

"This stuff is strong." She passed back the bottle and Veres placed it on the floor. Holding onto it for support, he turned himself around and sat up against the wall.

"Are we real? Do we really exist? Are we shadows in the dark or a figment of an imagination far greater than ourselves?" When drunk, some became aggressive, some depressed or happy, some even slept. Veres, on the other hand, became a philosopher. Better than a fist fight, though still as irritating.

"Well, at least you're not the violent type," said Karina. "For what do I owe this pleasure?" Veres wasn't listening. He hadn't finished. Did they ever. One-track minds.

"But does it matter? We exist, whether it's in some reality or not, and as such we must do what we have to do, what we feel we must or mustn't do, irrespective of whether there really is an existence because as we can 'see' that... there is... we are." He slowly took another swig from the bottle. It was almost dry, so he stared at its empty depths. "I've kept this for years. Now is the time to finish it." He passed it back to Karina. She declined. She felt its heavy percentage all down her throat, burning at her pipes.

"Thanks, but it might affect my... health," she said, tapping her head. *Running at 78% efficiency.* A little lower than usual. *Please do not ingest more of that 'contagion'.* Contagion? It's alcohol. You were okay with a beer or two.

"This is healthy!" he said, dropping the bottle. After another look, he let it go to roll away along the floor and down the corridor. Karina stood there and watched him for a while. He was lost in a little humming world of his own, his hands dancing to the music in his head.

"It's nice of you to pop in like this... well, I dunno about 'like this' but whatever. Was there something you wanted?" she asked. His eyes slowly locked onto hers. Could she see regret? Remorse? Was that a tear? He sneezed.

"We had to do what we had to do. There were no options. None. Stripped of all, enslaved by our own shame, impeccably numb." Was this a confession? Was he trying to confess something? Was this connected to what Puskash had said? Play dumb.

"What are you going on about, Veres?" His eyes left her, his head shook.

"What was done was done. The past is dead, the now is no more, the future... is here." A large shadow hung over Veres, catching Karina by surprise. It was Bohatch at the door. Veres lifted his head to the bull of a man in armour. With his laser rifle strapped on his back, Bohatch reached down and pulled up Veres.

"Sorry for this," he said to Karina. "He hasn't done this for a while." He looked over to the empty bottle. "Was that the last?"

"Yes, my dear sir, it was the last of many," replied Veres from under Bohatch's shoulder. "May God bless her and all who sail in her!" Bohatch shook his head at Karina.

"I'll take him back to his quarters," said Bohatch. He looked at the open door. "He opened your door in this state?"

"Err, yeah." said Karina.

"Okay, well, get back inside. The door will close after you," said Bohatch.

"Okay." Karina took a few steps closer to the pair who'd already started down the corridor. "I think he wanted to tell me something," said Karina. "I've been quite the listener recently."

"Later, maybe," said the guard. "Sorry about this. Good night, Miss Reif." And with that, they were gone. Veres was singing something that sounded like a little lullaby as he staggered down the corridor with Bohatch's help. Karina watched them go for a while and then went back into her room. Just as she went to hit the button to close her door, she felt a sharp pain in her right arm and turned her head to see the Doc's face before she lost consciousness, falling onto the floor of her room.

024

EMERGENCY reboot commencing in three, two, one...

Karina sucked in a breath and a bright, white light entered her eyes. Her head and neck pulled at restraints as she gasped for oxygen. "Where... where am I?" Her chest felt heavy and in pain.

"Excellent!"

She heard the Doc moving around behind her on some wheeled chair and coming close. A sharp pain shot through her brain and a cold, metal tool contacted her implant. "Ahh! What the hell are you doing?!"

"Uh-huh, I see..." A few more spikes of pain filled her head, increasing in intensity. "How about this?"

"Ahh!" Karina let out a scream as she almost lost consciousness. *Losing power. Transferring from backup supply. 36% power... 54% power. Running at minimal levels.* Karina heard a door open and footsteps tapping across the floor.

"Doc!" It was Puskash.

"Ah, Puskash! I'm just running a few tests," said the Doc. There was a melody in his voice.

"Puskash!" shouted Karina. "Help, he's trying to kill me!"

"What the hell do you think you're doing?" asked Puskash to the Doc.

"My dear boy! The 'woman' is over-reacting. I have to analyse the capabilities of the implant before its implementation," said the Doc. He was humming away quite happily now. Another metallic touch to her scalp sent pain into her skull.

"Ahh!"

"She's a human being, not a machine!" said Puskash. Karina couldn't see him or the Doc, everything was happening behind her. All she saw was a console on a wall filled with diagrams and graphs showing her life signs.

"Stop it!" she screamed.

"I would have thought of all the people here you would understand," said the Doc to Puskash. He humphed and moved on his chair again. "Without this implant 'she' is nothing more than a collection of non-responsive biological material." Was Karina really only dead meat? *Technically, you were brought back from the dead by the inclusion of the implant.* She felt so much better. Thank you for those kind words. *The truth hurts.* What are you, a meme?

"Yeah, but without 'her', the implant is useless," retorted Puskash. His face came into view as he inspected her face and looked into her eyes. He looked upset.

"What the hell do you think you're doing?" she shouted behind her to the Doc, pleading with her eyes to Puskash. "Let me out of here!"

"That is why I am running a few tests," replied the Doc, completely ignoring everything Karina had said. Another person entered the room. It was getting crowded in here.

"How's it going, Doc?" asked Viranyi. That was a surprise. It was the first time she'd seen... heard him outside his 'office'.

"Viranyi! Tell him to stop! Get me out of here! Puskash, help!"

"Well. Though it would go better without all these

interruptions." The Doc came into Karina's view and he pushed Puskash out of the way.

"It is quite imperative that you do your work. Yesterday was a close call," said Viranyi. So, if what Puskash said was true, those from the lower levels had attacked and made some damage. "We need the implant to be connected as soon as possible."

"What! Hello! I'm here! Speak to me!" shouted Karina.

"If he goes on like this, he's going to kill her!" said Puskash, now out of sight.

"Come now, Puskash! Have a little faith in the Doc. He's kept us all alive for decades. Do you think he wants to kill her?" asked Viranyi. Puskash went quiet while the Doc pricked and poked Karina's skull, usually accompanied with a shock.

"Ahh! Get him the hell off of me!"

"Wonderful. I think I'm now aware of all the biological precautionary procedures which must be adhered to before, during and after the implant exchange and substitution," said the Doc.

"How simple is it, Doc? To place the implant in?" asked Viranyi. What? Karina panted from pain and surprise. Place the implant in? They were going to kill her.

"It's not exactly 'Plug'n'Play', Viranyi. It is a gradual removal process from the biological vehicle which might take a few weeks, maybe months. There is also a chance that it may not work at all," informed the Doc. Karina tried to keep her senses awake. Were they really talking about killing her? By taking out the implant? That would certainly mean her death. *Affirmative.* Reassuring, as always.

"You can't do that!" she screamed.

"How about the technical side of things, Puskash?"

asked Vilayni. There was a pause. "Puskash?"

"There are some small interface problems, but nothing I can't handle," said Puskash in a quiet voice.

"Hey! I'm here!" Karina shook in her chair.

"Good. Before you do the deed, I would like to have a few words with our... guest," said Viranyi. "Alone." Karina heard Puskash shuffling out.

"Mmm?" asked the Doc.

"You too."

"Mmm? Oh, right. As you wish. She is secure," said the Doc, leaving. She heard the door closing behind them and Viranyi came into her view, placed a chair in front and sat down.

025

"WHAT the hell do you think you're doing?" She spat into Viranyi's face. He wiped it off with a handkerchief.

"What we need to do. Everyone has their place in their own time. Yours is to now supply us with a computer which can help us with our problems, irrespective of any other demands or wishes you may have, either personal or from society as a whole. Sadly our mainframe has seen better days and our need is greater than yours. To save the many you must sacrifice the few. Well, you, in this case. And your companion."

"You… you…" She was in one mind to tell Viranyi that Puskash had told her everything about those 'problems' and where the old man could stuff them. "You can't do this! It's unethical, it's… inhumane!" Is it possible? *Affirmative.*

He grabbed her by the shoulders and placed his face into hers. "They left us here to die! But we didn't! We survived, through whatever means possible! I'm not letting anyone stand in the way of our survival! At any cost!" He sank back into his chair, a little out of breath. "Yes, there were many times I was ashamed of what I did… I still am! But without doing what had to be done, we'd all be dead in this black hole of a mine!" He stood up and his walking stick appeared from his hand, helping him to pace over to a corner of the room. "A little more of the less, a little less of the more, that's what I used to say. Try and keep to the middle line, step light but step strong. Now… now I don't recognise those words coming from my own mouth. They're alien to me."

"You... you can't use me like this," she whispered. She wanted to say 'us' but as far as Viranyi was concerned, Karina knew nothing.

"People have been used since the beginning of time. If you listen to the Doc, a smart man though a little crazy, that was our main and only purpose, to be used. And he's not far wrong. Emperors and leaders used their citizens throughout history to do whatever they wished, religious leaders and politicians misled the masses to do as they wished. Tribes, races, gender, class... terms used against the masses to manipulate and use them for the wishes of those in power. And it goes on. AxiCorp continues to do as it wishes throughout the universe. And it will always go on so long as we live. This is the way of humanity. We are no different from those who came before us. As the Doc says, we were bred for it, made for it!"

"All I've been through, the virus, the... pain, this implant." Did he know about the vaccine? "And it comes to this? Used as a spare part in a crumby computer down a... a hole of a mine?"

"Yes, you have been through a lot, and now it's time for you to rest." He came back over and gently placed his hand on her left shoulder. "This, this implant must be like a curse."

"Like you wouldn't believe," she said. Was Puskash ready? She hoped Viranyi's words were as empty as his heart.

"It sure is an eyesore, too," chuckled Viranyi. How could he chuckle when he was about to execute her for 'the greater good'. He didn't speak for a while, which gave Karina some time to think.

"You would've just killed me right off, wouldn't you? If you thought the implant could've been taken without me?" Viranyi didn't flinch.

"We considered it. Puskash and the Doc interrupted our

plan to rip that computer from your head like we did with the shuttles..." said Viranyi.

"Shuttles?" What had they done? Puskash told her they only needed a computer.

"Yes. Some might say an unfortunate incident. As the elected leader amongst those who were left, I decided to strip what few shuttles we had of computers and connect them to the mainframe to keep the mine alive and running. I had to act quick, people were already dying from the failing system. And the shuttles were small, not big enough for everyone. It wasn't fair that a few could escape this mine, leaving the others to rot and die. So no one did, and there were no more deaths. For a while." So what Puskash said was correct.

"And when you've plugged in my implant, then what? I heard you have some trouble down below?" Would he tell her more?

"Trouble? Below? Who have you been speaking to?" asked Viranyi. He let go of her shoulder and sat back down.

"I think I know a laser fight when I see and hear one," she replied, to escape any retributions. "That was more than just a little 'argument' yesterday. It looked more like an all-out war!" He nodded his head.

"Yes. And that is why we need to use you. The system has been running down these last few years and with the extra processing power from the implant, we can regain parts that we lost control of, even gain parts we have forgotten we once had control of, and in so doing, take back the mine from those who wish to take it for themselves." A mouthful if ever there was.

"And who would they be?" She tried her luck.

"The monsters, of course." Monsters? What monsters? Viranyi stood up and walked behind her. "I'm sorry it had to end this way. It would have been nice to have had some new company around to talk to and spend time with, especially as you're a woman… in part." She heard him opening the door and the two other men entered. "I will leave you with those responsible for the procedure. Good day, Miss Karina Reif. I hope you will have a pleasant… rest from your pain." And he left, his stick tapping on the floor with an ever diminishing sound.

026

AS the Doc busied himself with collecting the tools and equipment for what he thought was about to happen — her eventual death, Bohatch came in holding a helmet. Puskash just stood at the door, resting on the frame. He looked pissed off. Had he had enough time to set things up the way he planned? By the looks of it, no. How was it going down? She didn't want to die.

"I've been told to give you this," said Bohatch, placing it on Karina's head and strapping it on. It was an old miner's helmet and the inside padding inflated to fit her head comfortably. "Viranyi said there could be trouble before you can be connected, or you might even have ideas while being moved. We need to protect your assets."

"And not my body? No armoured jacket?" she asked. "How do I look?" She leaned her head a little to the right to look cute, pushed her chest out and smiled. Although tied up, she was still able to place her hands on her hip. Bohatch didn't reply, merely stepping away with his head down.

"I have everything I need," informed the Doc. He was carrying a medical bag and dragging an IV pole on casters, ready for use with infusion bag and hanging tube. "Please unstrap the patient and escort her to the mainframe," he ordered. Bohatch did as he said and gently lifted Karina up.

She took her chance, as always — it was in her training, escaping Bohatch's gentle grip and rushed straight for the Doc, head first. She watched as the Doc came out of his thoughts and gave an expression of horror and surprise as she came closer, his eyes showing fear and the reflection of her metallic green helmet in his pupils. That alone was a fantastic bonus.

And nothing. The Doc's breath hit her eyelids. She hadn't made it, Bohatch had caught her in time. No matter how hard she struggled, she couldn't go even a millimetre more. "Ahhh!"

"Scream all you like, Miss Reif," said the Doc, right into her face — he had no choice. "The operation will proceed."

Bohatch pulled her away and through the door of the medical facility. They all marched down the dimly lit corridors to the control room which housed the mainframe, Puskash's place. No one spoke, all she heard were their footsteps, the occasional shout from the depths, and the squeaking casters on the IV stand. All this commotion for an implant. If only G.D. hadn't placed it in her head. If only he hadn't brought her back to life. If only she hadn't known G.D. at all! Then where would she have been? Probably dead, her body stuck in some unused tube down in the water installation back on Gubacsi for asking too many questions above her cut. Considering that, she had done all right for herself. Until now. Was Puskash ready? That was the big question.

The control room was dingy and tight, and a little smelly — possibly Puskash's body odour — so Puskash stayed outside while Bohatch strapped Karina into a chair. Because of the space, not the smell. He took off her helmet while the Doc placed the IV needle into a vein in her right arm. The Doc also stuck some more needles into her head, all connected to a portable monitor.

"I see your bedside table manner isn't improving," said

Karina, checking the straps by trying to punch and kick the Doc.

"I was never one for the 'shop floor', so to speak," said the Doc. Bohatch nodded to the Doc and left the room, allowing Puskash to enter the cramped area, who then closed the door behind him, leaving Bohatch outside. "I'm a scientist, purely that."

"So why the hell are you here, playing GP to a bunch of dumbass miners?" scoffed Karina. Puskash sat down to his desks and spun from one console to another, flicking switches and pressing buttons.

"I had a... disagreement with a colleague of mine. Research can get a bit stressful at times, especially when you are breaking the limits of science... and ethics, of course. Where would science be without ethics? I lot further, if you ask me."

"Next thing you're going to tell me is that you killed him," said Karina.

"My, Miss Reif, perhaps you should have gone into meteorology rather than police enforcement. Your prediction is correct. After the 'unfortunate' incident, AxiCorp transferred me here. I'm assuming they did not wish to waste my expertise, merely give me some... resting time." From his medical bag came an extremely long needle.

"What are you going to do with that?"

"Consider yourself lucky. Not many people nowadays have the opportunity to experience such pain. What a rich and exuberant life you will have had, Miss Reif." The Doc placed the needle into his left hand and pulled out a small drill with his right. "I just need to make a little hole in order to insert the needle into your interventricular foramen..."

"My what...?" The drill touched her skin on the back of her head and the bit turned. "Ahhh!" The Doc drilled straight into the back of her skull and pulled out the bit. Karina drew in a long, hard breath before she could speak. "No anesthetic, no nothing?! What kind of a doctor are you?"

"I told you, I'm a scientist, not a doctor. Now, keep steady..." No words could express what happened next as the Doc pushed the needle in. Okay, a few. She felt the initial push but then nothing. Karina's mind went numb.

"Are you done?" asked Karina. "I can't feel a thing."

"Exactly," said the Doc. "I strongly advice you don't move. It could result in damage to the surrounding tissue." Luckily, Karina could see everything Puskash was doing from where she was sitting without needing to move. "I am ready, Puskash. The first few minutes will be the most difficult but the body will settle down once the initial interface begins."

"Okay. I just need a few more minutes to calibrate and link," said Puskash. She saw the tablet, now sitting in his lap. Was the plan set? Had he enough time to work it all out?

"Where are the cables?" asked the Doc. "Or is there a wireless connection? I would have thought with all the processing and data transfer, you'd need a direct cable?"

"Yes, of course. That's the last thing. Give me a moment, will ya?" Puskash played with the tablet which Karina could see was directly connected to the mainframe.

"I see you have a new toy," said the Doc. He'd seen the tablet.

"This? Yeah, it was hers. It's pretty neat, quite efficient and easy to use. All the ones we had died years ago," said Puskash as he hit a few more buttons. He placed the tablet on the desk in front of him and stood up with two cables in his hands. "Got the cables. Ready to start once I connect these."

"Admirable," said the Doc. He looked down at his

remote console and checked the measurements. For Karina it was like watching a black and white B movie as the bad guy crept closer to his victim, and she was that poor, unfortunate victim. She imagined the cheesy crescendo music as he came closer... and closer, a cable in each hand, until... Puskash turned from Karina and placed the cables into either side of the Doc's neck. The Doc fell to the floor with a grunt.

027

"WE haven't got much time." Puskash quietly moved the Doc's body under a desk and went behind Karina. There was silence until she felt something metallic leave the back of her head. She began to fill a throbbing pain emanating from what felt like a large hole in the back of her head. "I'll put a plaster over that." There was more pain as he did so, but at least Karina didn't feel the wind blowing through her brain anymore. Puskash went back to his consoles. She was still tied up. "I've initiated the tablet into the system to give an impression that your implant is being connected, and I've opened up a few functions that haven't worked for a while in the mine so that the others think that we're making some progress. It won't work for long, though." He ran over to another console. "Recalibrating the cables for a connection. Rather than electrocution."

"That would be nice," said Karina. "Can you fill me in on what we're going to do, exactly? And?" She gestured to her restraints. Nothing.

"Yes… and no. I'm connecting you to the mainframe for a moment." He came back with the cables and secured them to her implant. "Anything?"

"Anything what?" *Connection achieved.* "Oh, yes, okay. I guess it's ready. Ready for what, no idea." She moved her body around to show Puskash that she was still tied up. Again, no acknowledgement.

"Don't worry, I only need its processing power for a few seconds. Hold on."

"What do you mean 'hold o…'" Her vision blurred and her head filled with a mass of light. *Inputting data.* No shit. Her head felt heavy. *Compressing.* What? The 'weight' grew denser until a pop of extreme white light appeared. *Exporting data.* I don't understand. What the hell is happening? Her vision came back to see Puskash deep in thought over a few of his consoles.

"Yes! It worked!" He stood up, shooting his arms in the air.

"What? What did you do?" she asked, confused.

"I just gave the colony another decade," said Puskash, smiling.

"What?"

"Your implant compressed the main database and simplified some major functions. I couldn't have done this without it." He hit a few more buttons and a surge of power rushed through her head. "Now all we need to do is…" The tablet started to smoke. "Oh crap!" Puskash touched its screen but jumped back, having burnt his fingers on his right hand. "Damn it!" With his left hand, he went over to a console. "Trying to disconnect the tablet from the mainframe… damn!" Karina saw the 'refreshing' icon playing over the console in front of Puskash. He grabbed some rag from under a few discs and held the tablet, pulling it off the cables. The console froze. "Shit!" Banging his fists on the desk, Puskash turned to Karina and unstrapped her from the chair. Finally!

"Why didn't you untie me earlier?" she asked.

"Sorry, wasn't thinking. Change of plan."

"What plan?"

"We have to move." Puskash scanned the room and picked up a few pieces of tech; cables, a few tools, and the Doc's portable monitor. "I can use this. Let's go."

The instant Karina stood up, the door swung open and

both Bohatch and Veres were standing there.

"What's going on? Just got a message from the first wave that there are no functions working on Level 18, 19 or 20," said Veres. "They've had to halt." First wave? Sounded like some assault or some… they were at war. Of course, they were going to use the surprise to attack their enemies. Both Bohatch and Veres had their laser rifles at the ready. Veres looked over the room and saw the Doc's body, under a desk. "What the hell did you do to the Doc?" Karina and Puskash were defenceless, none of them had a gun. Puskash put up his hands in surrender as Bohatch raised his rifle. Karina thought to do the same as Puskash, but couldn't be bothered.

Then a siren started in the distance. And then another. And another. The room lit up from a small flashing red light on the ceiling.

"The mainframe has collapsed," said Puskash. "Something went wrong with the Doc's side of things, we had to unplug and then…"

"Bamm!" said Karina. "He got a shock or something. I think he's dead." He and Karina looked at each other.

"What are you, a double act?" It was that obvious? "What now? Can't you reboot?" asked Veres.

"With the right equipment and a few hours, yes," said Puskash. "But now we're looking at a much bigger problem." The sirens continued as they stood there without a word. What was the problem?

"Hell. We're all dead," said Veres. "After all this time? You know, I told him!" he said, throwing his thumb behind him. "If it ain't broken, don't fix it! And now?"

"We can hide up in the top level, maybe Puskash can reboot from there with some remote connection or something," said Bohatch. Where was this coming from? Karina caught what she thought was a wink from Bohatch. 'Others', that's what Puskash had said.

"And then who's going to clear up the mess, eh? You?" asked Veres. Bohatch didn't answer. He just threw Karina the helmet.

"And what do I do with this?" she asked.

"Put it on. It might save your life," said Veres. "Okay, let's get up to the top level, see who's still around and go from there." Bohatch nodded and they both moved to leave.

"I... I have another idea," said Puskash. They all turned to him. "The shuttle bay."

"The what? Why the hell for? None of those shuttles work! You gutted them, remember!" shouted Veres. "Now, come on! We have to get out of here!"

"Why?" asked Karina.

"Because the bogey men will get ya," said Bohatch. Puskash wasn't moving.

"What now?" shouted Veres.

"I only gutted them of their computers," said Puskash. "Their turbines still work." He gestured over to Karina. The coin dropped pretty quickly for the other two.

"Lead the way, Bohatch! Get us to that shuttle bay!" shouted Veres. They all stampeded out of the control room and down the flashing red-lit corridors.

028

PUSKASH stayed behind Karina as they ran. They both let the other two go slightly ahead so they could speak.

"What the hell was Bohatch talking about? What's the problem?" asked Karina. "Is it the atmosphere? Are we going to run out of oxygen?"

"No, the mining facility is so vast that there's a huge amount of breathable air in here. It would take days, weeks before we ran out. By that time I could get the filters back online. No, that's not the problem." Explain away, nerd, just say what it is.

"Then what is?" They ran a whole corridor before Puskash replied. Was he out of breath or didn't he want to say.

"You said you saw the kids," said Puskash.

"Yes, I saw them." What was coming?

"Those were the Doc's successes."

"And his failures?" she asked. She knew the answer. Monsters. That's what Viranyi had said, the word 'monsters'.

"A lot of them died, but a lot didn't," he began. "They… they weren't so… civilised."

"What do you mean?"

"They had problems, either physical or psychological. The physical, they were mostly easy to assess and eliminate," he said.

"Eliminate? Kill them? But they're… you, aren't they?" Karina's level of disgust went up a few notches. These guys were the monsters, not… the 'monsters'.

"And? They're freaks, biological errors." Puskash made a face to show his contempt at Karina's question. "But the ones with only psychological problems, some chemical imbalance in the mind, now they were... troublesome."

"Troublesome?"

"We lost a lot of good men trying to control them out or get rid of them. And then Viranyi had the idea to herd them down to the lower levels and keep them there."

"Then what was all that you said earlier about a war?" asked Karina. Again, it took a while for Puskash to reply.

"Bullshit, sorry. I didn't want you to..."

"...realise what was going on here? Hell, Puskash, you're as far gone as the next guy!"

"I know, I know. None of us are perfect."

"Far from it! And what about the women?" Karina stopped running. "What about your daughter? Was that all bullshit too?" He stopped too and nodded.

"In part. The Doc has them all, even the ones unsuitable for fertilisation." Karina stood there, amazed. Just what was the truth anymore? And then it hit her. "What's wrong?"

"Borsodi! What about Borsodi? She's in here somewhere, ready to be a baby factory for you crazy idiots! Aren't we going to save her?"

"Well..." Puskash swayed his head in decisiveness. "She's being held in another part of the facility, far from here. We'd have to make a ton of diversions to get to her, and by that time, it would be too late."

"Too late for what? I'm losing my patience with this place! With you, Puskash! Too late for what?"

"With the mainframe down, the gates are released and...

'they' are free to roam. They'll be making their way up to the higher levels for food."

"Are you telling me you starved them as well?"

"No, we kept them on a strict rationing, but most of them have a... blood lust. For ours, mainly, seeing as we're the ones who put them down there."

"Monsters! Viranyi told me, monsters, he said." Karina pointed ahead, asking whether that was the way to go. Puskash nodded. "I'm wondering who exactly are the monsters here." She started running again, with Puskash in tow. The other two, Veres and Bohatch were nowhere in sight. "And what about your daughter?" she asked. Her head was filling with anger. Turning a corner, she wasn't paying attention and tripped on a jagged piece of metal, almost smacking her head on the far wall as she fell. A line of light shot past her head and she heard Puskash scream in pain. She watched as he hit the floor, too.

"Ah-ha! If it isn't Miss Karina Reif!" said Germann. He looked a bit shaky, but he was holding up a laser rifle.

"Germann! You shot me!" said Puskash. Karina kept her eyes on Germann and slowly shuffled over to Puskash. A hit on the shoulder. He'd live, but his left arm looked limp, not good for programming.

"I was aiming for her." He pressed the trigger again, but nothing happened. Karina made a move, but the guy dropped the rifle and flipped out a pistol. She held her ground, neither moving back nor forward.

"And what have I done to you?" she asked.

"What has she done, she asks! What haven't you done?" His face went red and his nostrils flared. "There was a status quo here and you destroyed it!"

"A status quo? This is what you call a status quo? A bunch of crazy miners using pseudo cloning for some kind of future? Is that it? Is that your idea of a life?" Karina thought of their options. *Few.* You're back. You're always off when the action is on. *Keeping your body alive. There are no feelings in my database but if there were there would be some resentment from your last comment.* Oh shut up, 'me'.

"Better than no life at all," said Germann, keeping his gun level with her head.

"And what about me? What about Borsodi? You were about to take our lives, mine for the implant, hers for her eggs." Germann's eyes widened as he realised someone had told her their dirty secrets. "You can't treat people like puppets and move them around wherever and whenever you want, change their lives for your own benefit! You can't mess with people's bodies like they're your own property!"

"Ah. You're fighting the wrong person. It's not me, it's none of us," said Germann. "Some people say life is like a chess game, we are pawns in a game. Some of us are stronger pieces, a knight, a priest, rook, even a king or queen but really we're all in someone else's game, no matter how we dress or behave."

"Why do all you guys talk in riddles," sighed Karina. She was sick of these guys!

"The real question is who's in charge of the board? Now that's where your fight is. The system that created me, you, everyone. Your fight is with the system, not me." He held the pistol stronger. "Do you play chess? If you do, make your move."

"My move?" Germann was still aiming the laser pistol right at her head. "Tell me, Germann, do you see much action?" Karina winked and smiled, trying to shake him.

"Action? Wha… what do you mean?"

"Looks like you need a bit more training."

"What? Why?"

"Your pistol has no charge and the safety is on," she said, pointing to his 'useless' weapon.

"Oh. Crap." He threw the gun at her and ran. Karina thought to run after him, but she remembered Puskash, bleeding on the floor.

"Can you walk?" she asked.

"Of course I can walk, he shot me in the shoulder," said Puskash. "I walk with my legs, not my arms."

"Then why are you still on the floor?"

"Because it was safer down here! Have you got a plaster?"

"Do I look like a doctor?" she said. Puskash got up and pointed down the corridor Germann had disappeared down.

"Not that one. This one leads to the shuttle bay."

029

IT wasn't exactly a short or easy way to the shuttle bay. Puskash led Karina in the wrong direction twice so they had to back pedal, and finally the implant woke up. *Second on the left, first on the right, up the stairs and first on the right.* So it's not too far, then. *Not finished yet.* Karina tugged on Puskash and dragged him on.

"Oh, yeah, now I remember... hey, how come you know the way better than I do? I've lived here for almost two decades," said Puskash. She pointed to her head. "Oh. You've got the map."

"Yeah. Great things, these implants. Not only do they come with a deathwish, they also have maps. And I heard you don't get out much." Karina followed the implant's directions, and then its next set, and then its next, until Puskash stopped her. "What now?"

"Can you hear that?" he asked.

"Hear what?" They both stood there silent in the red flashing light of the corridor. Along with the constant noise of the sirens, there was something, a faint sound of screams and howls echoing down the corridor.

"That," said Puskash.

"Who can't? Is it...?" Who would be screaming and howling? Only wild animals howled. The monsters. They were close.

"Probably."

Karina was concentrating so hard on those particular noises, she jumped when she heard a series of laser shots. "Lasers! Who is it?"

"We're all assigned one, so it could be anyone," said Puskash.

"Where's yours?"

"I lost it."

"How did you lose a laser?"

"I put it down on my desk and the next time I thought about where it was, it was gone," he said. She could believe him. Suddenly they heard heavy footsteps coming from the other direction and before they could turn, something pushed them both to the floor. Puskash gave out a cry as Karina landed on his bad shoulder.

"Where the hell have you been?" shouted Bohatch. "We've been sitting in that shuttle bay for ages! We can see the shuttles but they can't move! Not without you! We can't get off the planet without you! What's taking you so long?"

"We were waylaid," said Puskash.

"I can see that," retorted Bohatch. "Now, get going! People are waiting!" Bohatch helped them both up and started running down a corridor. Karina tried to follow but found herself out of breath. She bent at the waist and felt ill, her head dizzy. Too much stress for one night? "Hey! Reif!"

"I... I've found something," she said. Bohatch came running back.

"What? What d'ya find?" He looked down where she was looking.

"A rest," she replied. Bohatch stood up and paused for a moment, then ran down the corridor again. Got him. Karina took in a long, cold breath to calm herself down and ran, catching up with him. "Eh, Bohatch! What do you mean people are waiting? It's just you and Veres, no?"

"Not anymore," he replied. "We have a little...

company." They ran into the shuttle bay and were greeted by a dozen little white faces sitting together by a small shuttle. They looked scared, but most alarmingly, they looked young. The majority of them were children. Then she recognised them. They were the kids she'd seen, these were those kids. One of the boys pointed to her and said something to his closest neighbour. Viranyi was also there, with his head in his hands, sitting beside Veres. There was also someone else...

"Borsodi!" Karina was shocked. Of all the people to see, she was probably the last Karina had expected. "You're here!"

"Yeah, no thanks to you," she said. Her eyes were like daggers. What was wrong?

"How did you...? Where were you?" asked Karina.

"Like you gave a shit." Karina saw that Borsodi was covered in blood, her hair looked like some dark, matted heap on her head. She went over to her but Borsodi stood up and kept her distance. In her right hand was a laser pistol, and she held it tight. "Do you know what they did to me?" She pointed her gun at Viranyi's head.

"Where did you get that from? The pistol." Where was hers when she needed it?

"Oh, this? From a dead guy. Came in handy, too." She nodded over to the children. "I got as many as I could out before they came."

"They?" she asked.

"The monsters," whispered Viranyi.

"Took a few of them out, too, and now it's your turn." Borsodi lifted the gun up to Karina. This was getting to be a habit, people pointing a gun in her face. A really bad one. Maybe she should give it up, it definitely wasn't good for her health. Karina heard a few clicks as guns were being aimed.

Hopefully not at her but at Borsodi. But who could tell?

"Don't shoot!" cried Puskash. "She's the only chance we've got!"

"Her?" laughed Borsodi. "Look at her! She's a disgrace to her profession! She started the virus! Killed millions! They're still dying, every day more are gone! And now she's the only chance you've got!?"

"I didn't start the virus!" said Karina. "It was an... an accident!"

"An accident that killed my whole family, Karina." Borsodi put both hands on the pistol to steady her aim. "I was lucky, stationed off planet when the wave came through the sector. I didn't have to watch them die. But I survived." She was fuming. "I wasn't assigned to get you, I volunteered." That was news. "On one condition: that after they ripped you open like some lab rat on Farkas Alpha..." Where? "...I'd get to kill you myself. Slowly and painfully. But now... why wait." Borsodi sighted up her gun.

"No!" shouted Viranyi as he jumped up, getting in the way. In a split second, a searing heat surrounded Karina making her instinctively close her eyes... and then... silence. She felt a burn on her right shoulder, and as she opened her eyes, she saw it was more of a singe. Borsodi was still standing in front of her, the gun still aimed at her, but now the woman had a half-meter hole in her chest. She fell to the side and her gun let out a shot as her arms hit the ground, shooting aimlessly into the corridor behind. Another body lay beside hers. It was Viranyi. Bohatch, with a smoking laser rifle, rushed over to his body. They spoke for a few moments and Bohatch looked over at Karina.

"He wants to say something," said Bohatch. "To you."

Don't they all? Karina, gazing at the lifeless Borsodi, walked over to Viranyi. He too was hit, and badly. Blood oozed from the side of his mouth. He gestured her to come close.

"There is no meaning to all this. You get to a point where you have certain responsibilities either forced onto you or given by yourself through whatever means they came along and… you need to deal with them… until you die." And so he did. His words were… eloquent, for a dying man. Viranyi fell into Bohatch's arms, who lost his grip on his laser rifle and it hit the floor. Karina moved away from the two and back over to Puskash who was standing like a statue.

"Spoken like someone who died and came back with an implant stuck in their head," muttered Karina. "Are you okay?"

"No. I think I peed in," whispered Puskash.

"Keeping up with your stereotype, eh?" asked Karina.

"I am the stereotype," he said.

"And it's not a good example to show the kids, now, huh," said Karina. She checked herself. Other than the singe, she was unfazed by what had just happened, with her old Academy acquaintance, who they were going to use as a baby factory, trying to shoot her but die, and then the death of an old guy who'd saved her life. What was wrong with her? *Compensating stress overload.* Ah, the implant. See something, feel nothing. She knew a few people like that. And now was she like that?

The sirens shut off, causing everyone to halt in their actions, whatever they were, and listen, watching the corridors which led to the mine.

"What does that mean?" asked Karina.

"It means they're close," said Bohatch. "Puskash, choose a shuttle now!"

030

PUSKASH stood like a statue, gazing at one shuttle and then another. He wasn't helping. Bohatch physically pushed him towards them. There were only the two, one a little bigger than the other, but both open, with their ramps down. What was the problem?

"Stop it, I need to think!" shouted Puskash.

"Why?!" shouted Bohatch back.

"Which one would be easier to integrate with the implant... I'm trying to remember the circuitry." He pointed at them as though he was playing 'eeny, meeny, miny, moe'.

A noise came from down the mine. Howls. Distant. The children started to whine in distress and huddled together. Puskash took out the Doc's mobile console and went through some menus.

"We don't have time for you to play with your toys!" Bohatch's head was going red.

"That one!" Puskash pointed to the bigger one. "Get everyone on that one."

"Okay! Alright! A decision! Here we go, peeps, kids, go get on board!" Bohatch led the way and gestured the few miners who'd made it this far onto the open door ramp and into the shuttle. Puskash ran over to the side of the vehicle and opened up a small hatch, plugging in the mobile console and tapped away. Bohatch then pushed the group of about a dozen children onto the shuttle. "Well?" he asked Puskash, as he gestured for Karina to get onboard. "Come on!"

"Give me a moment, just get in and secure yourselves. We'll be there in a moment," replied Puskash as he waved Karina over to him. She went over and watched him working on the mobile console. What was he doing?

"Okay," said Bohatch. The howls were getting closer. "Make it quick!" Bohatch disappeared inside and Karina heard him shouting to the others to secure themselves into a seat. There was the sound of some commotion inside, definitely the kids, they were squabbling.

"Are they done?" asked Puskash.

"What do you mean? They're inside, like you said," said Karina. "Making some noise, though."

"Good." He tapped the console one final time and the open door ramp started to close.

"What the hell are you doing?" screamed Karina. She ran over and tried to catch the end of the ramp but her fingers slipped off the end. "You closed us out!"

"No, I closed them in. They're safe now. We can remote control their shuttle once I connect you to the other one." Puskash pointed over to the second, smaller shuttle.

"What?"

"Come on, you don't want to travel with kids, do you? Really? They can be a pain." Puskash shoved the console into the hatch and closed it up. "We can remote connect to this." The howls were now incredibly close. "One more thing!" He ran over to a large pipe by the wall. "Can you help?"

"With what?" Karina looked back at the noises coming from the corridors leading to the bay.

"With this valve!" She ran over and they both pulled on a lever and were able to move it. "Good! Now let's go!" He ran over to the second shuttle. Karina didn't have a choice.

As they stepped onto the open door ramp of this shuttle,

Karina saw in the corner of her eye some movement, a flickering of light at the corridors which led from the mine. They'd arrived. The monsters. She could now only hear her steps on the metal ramp as they ran into the shuttle, loud, echoing. Puskash pressed the button to close the ramp. Nothing happened.

"Shit!" exclaimed Puskash.

"What's the matter?"

"No computer, no power!"

Manual control. What? *To the right. Lever.* "Quick! Help me!" Karina could see it, a small red lever to turn anti-clockwise to close the ramp. Another lever? Puskash ran over and they both cranked it around and around. It wasn't easy, but the ramp was closing fast. There was only about half a metre left to close when two hands appeared on the end of the ramp. Hands, well, something similar to hands, more like lumps of meat with a few sticking out bits, but what else could they be? Feet? *Pistol. Eight o'clock. On the wall.* What? Not this clock shit again! *Behind you, down.* She saw it, and left Puskash to turn the lever. Grabbing the pistol and switching the safety off, she fired at the 'hands'. They disappeared with a scream. How do you know so much about this shuttle? *Standard AxiCorp transport shuttle third class.* Oh. Right. Do you think you can fly this thing? *Can fish swim in the ocean?* Not anymore they can't, what with pollution and mass garbage dumping. *Bad analogy. Affirmative.*

"Closed!" said Puskash, catching his breath. He jumped back in fright as the outside of the shuttle was hit by a crowd of... whatever it was out there.

"Can they get in?"

"Nah, they're strong but they're not superhuman. It just made me jump, that's all. Too much excitement for one day."

The monsters outside bashed against the metal fuselage with futility. Karina guessed they were doing the same with the other shuttle. "Okay, I have to... plug you in." They rushed up to the cockpit and Puskash pulled out the cables he'd brought along.

"Is it going to hurt?" she asked. She saw Puskash pause.

"To be honest, I don't know. Did it hurt when I connected you to the mainframe?"

"A little." Karina sat down on one of the two pilot seats.

"Can you take it? The pain?" he asked, while removing the helmet.

"When have I not?" she said. Puskash nodded his head and connected the cables first to the main console of the shuttle and then to her implant. Puskash sat down on the other pilot seat and looked at her. "Now what?"

"Oh." He faced the console and hit a button. Heat filled her head. *Connection achieved.* Good. Is this how hot it's going to get, or is there more? *Compensation measures activated. Side effects may appear.* What side effects? Silence. What side effects?! "Hey, we're on!" The console began to light up. "Okay, everything seems fine. First this." Puskash flashed through a menu and hit a button. A few seconds later the shuttle rocked, but then steadied itself.

"What was that?"

"You should know," he said. She did, the implant told her. He'd opened up a water valve on the Gubacsi Dulu water shuttle above them on the outside landing bay, which was connected to that valve they'd opened a few moments ago. The rocking was the water pouring through the shuttle bay and down into the depths of the mine. "That'll keep them busy for a while." Had he just infected the whole mine with the virus? At the least he'd flooded the place, gave them a good wash. "I'll open a channel to the other shuttle." By this point, Karina was feeling light-headed and relaxed. She sat back and sunk into the cushion of the seat.

"I haven't felt like this for a while," she said with a smile.

"Uh-huh." Puskash switched on the comms. "Bohatch? Bohatch!" There was a pause but the familiar voice came through.

"What are you doing, you piece of shit?!" shouted Bohatch.

"I thought it would be better to take both shuttles," he replied. "Remote connecting now. Out."

"I'm gonna kill you, you fu…!" Bohatch was cut off.

"Nice guy when you get to know him, eh?" asked Karina. Her head shook as the second shuttle's systems connected. She hiccupped. "Ooops, sorry." Puskash looked at her.

"Are you okay?"

"Fine." These side effects were interesting. *Compensating. Chemical and hormonal compounds administered.* Thank you.

"Well…" Puskash ran his hands across the console like a pianist playing the ivories. "Systems running at standard levels. Looks like we can go."

"Where to?" asked Karina.

"Ah, now there's a question," said another voice from behind them.

037

KARINA swung around in her seat — the cables flapped against the side of her head — and saw... she had no idea. Who was this? She recognised the uniform. AxiCorp state official.

"Klemm!" exclaimed Puskash. Yeah, that was the name. The company guy. A right pain in the arse, if she remembered the description from Viranyi... the old guy was gone. She felt a little sad... but hey, she didn't know him well. Now, what's going on? Other than this inconvenience of someone else in the shuttle, she felt like she was floating on a cloud.

"I see you have the consignment," said Klemm. Consignment? She'd met these words before.

"Yes, sir," said Puskash. Sir? What was this, another trap?

"Where did you come from?" she asked. "Is this your place?" She looked around the cockpit. "Could've cleaned up at bit."

"No, no, Miss Reif. It's all part of the plan," said Klemm, giving a toothy smile.

"Oh hell, not again," she sighed. "Are you telling me you're working for the company?" she asked Puskash.

"I always was. Isn't everyone?" replied Puskash.

"Does she have the vaccine, too?" asked Klemm. He knew about the vaccine?! Hang on, step back — Puskash knew about the vaccine?! That's not what he'd said.

"Yes, it's stored in her implant in code. I have yet to break it but that is only a matter of time," said Puskash.

"Excellent! Here are the co-ordinates," said Klemm, passing his wrist over to show Puskash his comms.

"Okay, thank you, sir." That 'sir' stuff was grating.

"So you set me up?" she said to Puskash.

"Kind of," he smiled. "Am I still going by stereotype?"

"You've just moved from one to another," she replied. "I liked the first one better. I guess the next thing for you to do is to strap me down."

"Would you like that?" Klemm was standing back now, with a pistol in hand. How many times had she been under the gun today? It was becoming a bore. "It can be arranged."

"I think it's best," said Puskash. Karina tried to stand up and she grabbed Puskash but got a shock. He was much stronger than she thought. He pushed her back down into the seat and wrestled with her until he had strapped her left hand to the armrest. She wasn't able to headbutt him but Karina somehow got her right loose and went for the cables on her implant. Without a connection, they weren't going anywhere. Puskash was faster, though. Her right hand was soon strapped down, too. She spat in his face. "Now who's doing stereotype?"

"You're full of shit! All that talk about getting away, and... and what about your daughter? That was all bullshit, too!"

"Not precisely," interrupted Klemm. Puskash ignored Karina and began to work the shuttle's console. Shut down connection. Unable to comply.

"What do you mean?"

"We all have sons and daughters here, who do you think those creatures out there are?" The banging on the fuselage had long since stopped. They were all probably trying to wade back through the water. "Each one of us has our fair share of offspring. And some of them are on the other shuttle, completely healthy children. Talking of which, we should send them off to the nearest colony, Puskash."

"Yes, sir." Puskash got busy on the console. "Connecting remotely. Once I've sent the co-ordinates and set the turbines, we can let the mobile console control them."

"You know best, Puskash, I know nothing of these things," said Klemm.

"Where are we going?" asked Karina, feeling the pull of more processing inside her head. *Connection acquired.*

"To the closest AxiCorp installation. From there we can relay the vaccine once decoded and all will be well," replied Klemm.

"What, you'll stop the virus by making the vaccine available to the population?" At least some good would come of this.

"What? And miss out on the profit? Are you insane?" Not so difficult to answer. "Do you know how much this vaccine could make on the open market?" Klemm asked. "More than any other business venture we have! Your implant holds a fortune! Ha!"

"Shuttles are ready to go, sir," said Puskash.

"Proceed."

The turbines started turning and Karina's head buzzed. It wasn't a bad feeling, but it wasn't nice, either.

"The other shuttle is ready to go," said Puskash. "Punching in the co-ordinates."

"Where are they off to?" Puskash showed Klemm their destination. Karina already knew, and it meant nothing to her, just a bunch of numbers. "Ah-ha. I heard the weather's quite warm there."

"The fauna isn't too friendly, though, sir. But it is the closest colony," said Puskash.

"Good, good." The shuttle lifted from the bay floor and they started moving forwards. Karina knew the other shuttle was ahead of them, already leaving through the bay doors and moving into orbit. They broke through into the outside world and began to ascend. "Send a message to AxiCorp, Puskash. Tell them we're coming."

"Yes, sir, once we've cleared the atmosphere," said Puskash. "We'll get a comms connection from there."

"Of course, of course, no rush," said Klemm. Karina had a thought. Which wasn't one about running two shuttles.

"You know that you're all crazy, don't you?" she said.

"Why, yes, of course!" said Klemm. "Becoming crazy was a needed evolutionary change in our psyche to survive. And we'll do it again, just to survive. That's what it's all about, isn't it? No matter what happens, keep on moving, forwards, backwards, sideways, whichever. MTSG!"

"MTSG!" repeated Puskash with a smile and a salute.

"You see, you're all crazy."

"Ready to release remote control of the other shuttle," said Puskash. Klemm nodded. Karina felt another pull, sending the right side of her head down.

"Woah, steady on, Puskash," said Karina. "I might pull a muscle or something."

"That… wasn't me," he said, flashing across the shuttle's controls. "There's something wrong…"

"What is it, Puskash? Come now, speak up!" commanded Klemm.

"I can't seem to disconnect the remote, sir, because… it's already disconnected." Puskash busied himself with one console. "I… I don't understand."

"I do," said Karina, her neck straining to the right. "They made a connection from the shuttle themselves." She felt a little strange, like she'd drunk too much. Just a little queasy.

"What? Impossible! They'd have to... I dunno... how is that possible? Oh no," sighed Puskash. Klemm grabbed hold of the console Puskash was working on.

"What is it? What is it!"

"They've changed course," said Karina. "Heading this way." Puskash's nose grew. Little liar.

"How?" asked Puskash.

"Set the course! Set the course!" shouted Klemm.

"I'm trying, I'm trying!" shouted Puskash.

"You can't." Karina's head came back up. "Someone on that shuttle has gained control." She felt it. Someone had hacked into her implant. Who? Karina watched as a kaleidoscope of butterflies slowly fluttered through the cockpit and out the main screen, into the sky and above. *Compensating. Balance achieved. Side effects may vary.* What? The comms came to life.

"Hey there, Puskash! It's Bohatch! One of these kids hacked into Karina's implant. You know what? I'm coming for ya! And I see you, Klemm! MTS bloody G! Salute that one! Hope you're ready for some action!"

032

KARINA watched the two guys running around the shuttle like headless chicken: Puskash was pressing every button possible, sometimes bashing them, other times hitting them with his head, while Klemm was trying to get the comms open — he didn't have a clue, screens flashed red and blue throughout the cockpit. Chaos.

"Nothing works!" shouted Puskash.

"Help me get a message out!" screamed Klemm. Puskash stopped what he was doing and went to help the idiot.

"We haven't left the atmosphere yet, so it's going to be tricky, but I can't even get the damn thing to work!" said Puskash, again banging his fists on the console. Karina knew the other shuttle was getting closer, and it had turned around, facing backwards. *Ramp opening.* What? She saw it in her mind's eye. Both shuttle ramps were opening, in the air. Surely that was dangerous.

"Sir! The ramp!" They both swung around to see the dark, stormy sky appear.

"Oh hell!" Klemm took out his laser pistol while Puskash strapped himself in. The ramps were half open when the shooting started. Klemm went nuts, shooting everywhere he could as though he were a blind man. The shots from the other shuttle, presumably Bohatch, were fewer in number and much more accurate, hitting consoles and cables. Some of Klemm's shots hit their own shuttle while the others flew out of the open ramp into empty sky. "Puskash! Can't you do anything!" He continued to shoot. "Puskash!" No answer. Karina looked over to where he sat. There was a small hole through the back of his seat. He was slumped forward.

"I think he's dead," said Karina. A quiet end for a devious nerd.

"Damn it!" Klemm kept shooting, but the shuttle jolted left and right and his aim became more erratic, now mainly hitting the inside of the shuttle. Tiny explosions and fires erupted throughout the cockpit. One large jolt forwards threw Klemm to the back of the vehicle... and out. Gone. And like that, Karina was alone.

"Reif!" It was Bohatch on the comms.

"Yeah?"

"Are you still in one piece?"

"I never really was in one piece, but yeah, I guess so!" She looked over her body. No laser holes, miraculously. The shuttle's movement grew smoother.

"I'm going to try and board!"

"Okay!" Karina watched as the fires grew in the cockpit. The console popped and sizzled and suddenly the shuttle fell from the sky and her stomach jumped straight into her throat.

"Reif!"

The feeling of weightlessness as the shuttle fell was too much, the g-force was starting to make her lose consciousness.

"Reif! We're disconnecting! Reboot! Reboot!" shouted Bohatch. *Connection lost. Reboot in three, two...*

Karina's eyes opened wide. What's going on? A console came to life in front showed a view of outside. The shuttle was flying through clouds, there was a storm below and smoke all around her.

"Reif! Reconnect! Reconnect! We're losing altitude!

...Karina!" Bohatch's voice screamed through the comms. *Unable to reconnect. Damage to remote sensors. Time needed: three hours forty-two minutes and...* They're falling! *Unable to reconnect. Damage to remo...* How about the comms? They're working? *Insufficient data transfer capability for full connection.* Full? *Partial connection is possible.* So? What are you waiting for? Their deaths? *Reconnecting through comms.*

"Bohatch! Bohatch! Can you hear me? I'm trying to reconnect you through the comms! Something's damaged here! Bohatch!" *Unable to respond due to comms system usage.* Damn! So what's happening other than my head burning up like toast? *Able to slow their descent.* Will they survive? *It is possible. Calculations are unavailable at this present time.* Where will they land? At the mine? *Insufficient control to change landing destination. Approximately three hundred and twelve kilometres from the mine.* That was 'approximately'? How will they survive without shelter? They said the conditions outside were hazardous to health! Hell, I even know that! *Their shuttle is fitted with emergency habitat units and rations. If all passengers survive the landing, they have enough food and water for fifteen days. Once out of the atmosphere, you can jettison a beacon which, if working efficiently, will show their position to any shuttle passing by within fifty light years.* Great. And what if no shuttle passes by that close? *Then they will not survive. That is why the beacon's accumulator's end-of-life will be set for twenty days, thus boosting its range to one and fifty.* Still not much of a range. Why not fifteen days? *A human can survive without water for up to five days. Without food, four weeks but water is essential for life, as you are aware.* Water. So precious to life. Ironic in their present state of affairs. She'd found out the horrific truth about the water humanity had been drinking for... who knew how many years, decades, maybe longer. And on top of that now she'd also found a small colony of miners so lost they'd started re-creating themselves with some pseudo clone/vitro fertilisation method. Both were done for survival, and both were acts of sickening evil, against all human rights, to keep a society alive, no matter how large or small, no matter how sick, demented or deranged. Where had all the virtue gone? Karina received the information, the other shuttle had landed. *Comms available.*

"Bohatch! Bohatch! Are you there?" No reply. Are the comms working? *Affirmative.* "Bohatch!"

"Here! Hell, Reif, I've been trying to get through to ya! Where were ya? I dunno how but somehow we came down almost as light as a feather!" shouted Bohatch over the screams and hollers in the background. The kids were going wild with fright.

"I couldn't reconnect properly, I had to go through the comms! Glad you made it!" Was she? He was one of them, one of the demented. There was one thing, at least more didn't have to die, there'd been enough already. "Is everyone okay?"

"One kid got a broken arm, and one of the guys got cut up badly, but nothing else except some bumps and bruises." There was some louder shouting in the background. "Hey! Cut it out! If any one of you little shits hit another button I'm gonna shove you right out the air lock!" It quietened down. A little. "What now? Are you gonna come down and get us?"

Insufficient capacity in this shuttle. Yeah, well how about swapping over to theirs? *The 'feather-like' landing damaged most of the shuttle's main systems. Able to reattach temporary life support system before disconnection.* So, no go? *Affirmative. It is not advisable to exchange.*

"Bohatch!"

"Yeah?"

"There's no room," she said. Those words were weak. She twitched at her own uselessness.

"What?"

"I can fit..." *Seven.* "...seven of you..." *Six.* "...sorry, six of you," she replied.

"That'll do!" said Bohatch.

"Who do you leave behind?" Bohatch went silent. Who do you leave behind?

"Then what?"

"Apparently you've got supplies there, and some habitat units." The comms were open but nothing was coming through. Was he thinking?

"You're joking, right?"

"I'll send out a beacon to call for help!" Again, the words sounded weak and the comms went silent for a while.

"You piece of... to who? Who's gonna help us?" Bohatch roared. Another long silence. "How long have we got?" She didn't want to reply. "Reif! How long have we got?"

"Fifteen days, maybe twenty." The comms went dead. Not silent, dead. And she guessed, for all their chances, so were they. Can we help in any way? *There are no supplies on board this shuttle. Do you wish to stay and help?*

She had to think about that one. What was important? She was alone, free, inside a working shuttle, cruising through the storm clouds of a remote planet stricken off the company's charts. What, no food? *There are some ration bars.* A compartment flung open at the back of the cockpit and a few fell out. Drink? *There are some bottles.* Bottles? That meant... her mind went back to Gubacsi Dulu, the truth, the virus, the need for a solution. She had the vaccine. In code. *Unable to give resources to decryption due to possible systems overload.* Overload? *Possible.* Anything else to drink? *Considering the possibility that the bottles of water are contaminated, there is only one other liquid which can be drunk.* Beer? *Negative.* Is it what I think it is? *Affirmative.* Gross.

Karina looked around the cockpit and realised she was stuck in her seat. At least help me with these straps. *Affirmative.* Her head dropped as power in her enhancement suit went to her arms. She ripped off the straps and power was redistributed so she could lift her head. Thanks. What now? A safe place, maybe? *Calculating coordinates.* What? To where? *Somewhere safe.* There's a place that's safe? *Possible.* Is it close? *You will need to eat the ration bars.* Yuck. *And drink your...* Thanks, yeah, I got it.

She sat back in her seat, watching the shuttle fly over the clouds and into space and gave herself a moment to rest, to think. Until she saw Puskash slumped in the other seat.

"Puskash?" She had to check. With a slow push, she shoved his body off the control board and let it fall to the floor, giving a thump as it contacted with the metal grid below. And that was the last sound she heard. The silence began to hit her until it felt like a ten ton concrete block resting over her head. What was it all about? She'd been walking around, sitting, listening to a bunch of crazy guys, and girls, for days, weeks... Everything that had happened, had happened TO her, with very little choice on her part since the implant... no, before that, well before that. Her job, the bribes, the placement, even the Academy — she was forced to join, had no alternative — and her education...? Everything. She'd never been in charge of her own life, never. Someone or something had always been there to push her in one direction or another. Sure, she'd made decisions, which door to try, which one to walk through and which one to leave closed, but who had showed her those particular doors in the first place? The drink, the drugs, the money... they'd all blinded her to the truth: no freedom, no free will. She was just like the rest of those poor unfortunates being pushed to their deaths to create wealth for those few in power. But was that all life was? Enslaved to those in need of money and power, death and poverty for the masses, genocide and massacre to quench the thirst of the rich. Literally. Was it time for her to find another way?

"Oh, for a Boroka357." Even with the knowledge, the craving, or memory of it, was still there, begging, pleading. *It is not advisable.* Bloody implant. *As I am connected to your brain, I can activate certain nerve cells to create natural neurotransmitters to send messages similar to those given to you by this drug.* Oh, it's 'I' now? Sorry, you can what? *Like this.* ...Wha...wha... what was that? *That was an o...* I know what that was! "Oh, I feel violated." She moved around in her seat. And you didn't even take me out to dinner or anything. *Strictly speaking, that was a form of mas...* Enough already. *Affirmative.* No, I mean, with the talking. *Affirmative.* She made herself comfortable. Long flight, eh? *Affirmative.* Bring it on. *The...?* Affirmative. *What about the dead body on the floor?* You had to go and ruin it, now wouldn't you?

AFTERWARD

Thank you for reading Radnoti X, the second part of Humanity H2O!

Please don't forget to write an honest review of the book on Amazon - reviews are the food of writers, without them we wither and die like a rose in the sand.

If you haven't read the first part, or would like to recommend it to a friend, then what are you waiting for?

Best Regards,
Dani J. Caile
http://danijcaile.blogspot.com/